PRAISE F

'...what an e
stories is a skill all in itself, and this collection of tales were very well crafted and told so much with a sparseness that was elegant and precise.'

JULIA BLAKE,
multi-genre author of ten novels and
one short story collection

'...there is plenty of the unexpected to be found in these tasty morsels! Hanson provides a smorgasbord of short and micro fiction, each leaving you with something different to chew on. Many of the stories have a deliciously uncomfortable edge, but my favorite is The Performer because of its beautiful prose and endearing romance.'

NANNETTE KREISMAN,
short story author

'...In his wonderful, eclectic collection of stories, Bruce Hanson has illuminated the gamut of human experience and emotion: the joy, pain and angst of love, insanity, conflicting values, selflessness, courage, hypocrisy, hope, abuse, and more. His work not only entertains, but raises a mirror to our own selves and the lives we live. Hats off, ladies and gentlemen. This book is a rare achievement in creativity, craft, insight and sensitivity.'

RAYMOND HOLMES,
author of Witnesses and other short stories and
A Barber's Son – Recollections of growing up in
1950's Toronto

MURDER & OTHER LOVE STORIES

Thought provoking suspense
with twists of the dark side

A Collection of Short Fiction

By

Bruce A Hanson

SML Books

Copyright © 2023 Bruce A Hanson
Individual Stories Copyright © 1996-2020 Bruce A Hanson

All rights Reserved.
ISBN: 978-1-9990095-4-0

No part of this book may be reproduced in any manner except in the case of brief excerpts in critical reviews and articles. The use of any part of this publication reproduced, transmitted in and form or by any means, electronic, mechanical, photocopies, recorded or otherwise, or stored in a retrieval system, without prior written consent of the author is an infringement of the copyright law.

Art Work
Photograph of The Fascinator, 2015 sculpture by Sally Thurlow Copyright © 2015 Ian Mackay. The photograph is reproduced herein with permission of Ian Mackay reproduced and Sally Thurlow.
Artwork of Twins is by, and reproduced with permission of, Karrie Barnum.
Photo of the Electra 12A aircraft was taken in June 1955 ar Helsinki-Malmi Airport in Finland. Photographer unknown. It is used herein under the Creative Commons Attribution 4.0 International license.
All other photos are by Bruce A Hanson

Earlier versions of some stories in this collection have been previously published as follows:

'Twins' in Wordscape 6 - Mystery and Suspense and in Unleased Ink 2;
'The Saviours' (under the title 'The Saviour') in Winners Circle 10;
'Daddy's Home' in CanWrite! - Short Story Anthology
The Order and The Dreamer in Unleased Ink 2
'The Unknown Civilian on the Muskoka Authors Association web site

The content and characters in this book are fictional. Any resemblance to actual persons or happenings is coincidental.

Murder & Other Love Stories

Includes Award Winning Stories:

Twins
The Saviours
The Unknown Civilian
Daddy's Home
The Collector

Table of Contents

Twins	1
The Salesman	13
The Order	47
The Saviours	53
The Unknown Civilian	71
The Performer	77
Daddy's Home	137
The Artist	147
Swimming	151
The Dreamer	159
The Marksman	175
The Collector	199
Body Art	221
In Conclusion	223
Author's Notes	225

TWINS

"When we were younger, we used to talk for hours…"
Sketch by Karrie Barnum

TWINS

My body was numb. My brain throbbed with excruciating pain. Women shouted obscenities and banged on the bars. The prison guard dragged me up and flung me into the cell. My legs wavered. No support. I didn't feel my knees strike the floor. My palms slapped concrete.

"Come on lady, it isn't that bad," the guard said. "You'll get used to them."

The heavy door slid into place with a dull clang. I shivered at the sound.

"I'll never get used to them," I sobbed.

Hopelessness choked out my voice. My eyes struggled to contain the tears as another surge of fear, wrapped in hate, screamed inside of me.

The judge didn't believe me. My parents didn't believe me. No one believed me.

The voices outside the cell hooted and hollered again. How could anyone in here find anything to laugh at? But of course, they were laughing at me.

My vision blurred.

"Hey, skank. Come here often?"

"What a grody hoe!"

Their vile words burned like dripping acid.

"You're a charmer. Why don't you stay awhile?" The voice cackled with laughter.

"She's a freak! Did you look at her? What a shit mop. Who's your hairdresser?"

I watched the guard, Shannon, turn her back to me and yell, "Keep it down. Let your new neighbour get adjusted."

"I'll adjust her for you, Shannon," whined another.

Shannon pushed her hands out in front of her as if she was brushing aside invisible branches, or maybe trying to wave away some stench. "You dolls have one hell of a welcome wagon."

A rotund woman in the opposing cell stood watching me. Her pounds of flesh divided into thin sections by the heavy grey bars between us. When she spoke, the others fell silent.

"What's your name, sweetie?"

"Jeannie," I wheezed.

"Well Jeannie, tell Aunt Flo why you're here."

"They said I killed my boyfriend. That I murdered him. But I didn't do it." My stomach ached. I gagged.

"Why won't anyone believe me?"

A few voices murmured. Maybe some of them shouldn't be here either. Maybe we can help each other.

"Why did they believe my sister and not me?"

The large woman took the bars in her fleshy grip. "For the same reason they didn't believe me, dearie."

She threw back her head, cackled and boomed out, "Cause I was lying. Just like you, ya dumb, screwed up little bitch."

Raucous laughter erupted and twisted through the bars, colliding with my eardrums, setting them ringing. I clamped my hands to my ears and wailed.

I couldn't raise my eyes from the floor, so cold, grey and lifeless—like the remaining fragments of my life. Of course they were laughing at me, just like Brigitte would be laughing at me this very minute. That bitch. Listen to me—starting to sound like her. Brigitte's laughing, all right. Me here and her free. Me, starting to sound as gross and crude as her. She'd like that. The bloody, murdering bitch.

I sat back on my heels, taking slow, deep, quivering breaths. The heckling died down.

A warm hand clasped my shoulder. A voice behind me whispered. "Tell me about it."

In a plea for understanding, I continued to reveal my painful past. "She stole the only man I'd ever loved, ever touched, ever…then killed him, slaughtered him, so I could never have him again. Sliced him horribly to destroy my memory of his gorgeous face."

Images flooded back—pictures of the coroner pulling back the sheet, the pale skin, the dried blood, the slices, red, puffy, stained, the once-beautiful face—

mutilated…. 'No, he had no enemies that I know of…. No, I have no idea who did this.'"

I wiped the wet from my eyes and nose.

"I didn't know who had killed him. It wasn't until she told me. Brigitte wanted me to know that she'd ruined my life."

I took another long breath.

"I can't count all the times Brigitte hurt me, embarrassed me, all the times she hated me for being alive. I was the one who should've been jealous. Our parents loved her. Not me. It was her picture in that album they kept. Her baby picture hanging under the cross in the living room." I paused, trying to stop my voice from wavering. "She was so cruel, but no one saw it. No one believed me." My teeth clenched. I forced the words out. "Our parents never blamed her. She was perfect. She was an angel.

"Oh, I wasn't alone. Brigitte bullied other kids too, but she saved the best of her warped mind for me. 'I was special,' she said."

Another hand touched my other shoulder. "Come and sit down."

I tilted my head back. A worn and harsh face looked down on mine. The eyes sat on small, dark pillows. Inside those eyes was a soft presence.

She helped me up. I leaned on her as we moved to one of the two sagging cots in the cell. I hadn't noticed the sink or the open toilet until then, stained and standing starkly against a grey wall.

"I'd watch my back if I were you, Mitch," croaked the fat woman in the cell across from ours. "This one's psycho. Trust me. I've seen 'em all."

"Go back to your knitting, Flo. Give her a chance."

My cellmate's gentle touch and comforting voice were like balm for my nerves. "Thank you," I managed to say.

She moved to face me. "Sounds like you've had a rough time of it. I've been in here for nine years, and that's because some bleeding hearts worked hard to get me off death row." The corners of her lips turned up slightly. "I've come to realize this isn't such a bad alternative. You were right, though; you don't get used to them, or this place. No one does, not completely. You can learn to live with it though. Even Flo over there isn't so bad once you warm up to her."

"Th-thanks. I…I…"

I meant thanks for listening, but the words stumbled and stuck on my tongue. She smiled and asked me about myself.

We talked for hours, my life spilling out as if we were in a private room rather than a cell where everyone could hear.

I told Mitch about my relationship with my twin sister Brigitte. When we were younger, we used to talk for hours, lying on our bed, listening to music and giggling. I described all the great times we had together and the terrible times that grew out of them. How, in the last few years, Brigitte had started telling me in advance that she was planning to hurt me, to punish me. She manipulated my emotions until I lived in total fear, knowing something was going to happen but not knowing what or when.

"I remember one dreadful morning like it was yesterday. She woke me up, smirked and rolled over on her side of the bed. I almost threw up when I saw what she had done.

"I stood in front of the mirror and broke down. My beautiful, shoulder-length auburn hair. The only thing about me that was gorgeous. The one thing I had that she didn't. And it was gone. That terrible morning, when I looked in the mirror, and instead of my wonderful hair, there was a field of weeds. Ragged, roughly-sheared tufts. She had butchered my hair while I slept.

"Our parents wouldn't believe Brigitte would do such a thing. They said I did it. That I did this to myself. Why would I destroy one of the few things I liked about myself? Brigitte sat there with her sweet innocent smile."

I ran my fingers across my scalp. "I decided to keep my hair the way she cut it. I wanted to show her that I could take her sick jokes, that I was stronger than her, independent of her. She couldn't survive without me to abuse, but I could survive with or without her. Every Tuesday night from that time on, I cut it myself, different lengths everywhere. Now, I personalize it. Every week, I dye the tips different colours, just to annoy her."

I mentioned the last conversation I had with Brigitte, something I hadn't revealed to anyone because I had learned no one would believe me. I repeated the exact words Brigitte whispered in my ear before they hauled me away to this place, the exact words she spoke so tenderly while hugging me for the entire world to see but not hear. "Dearest sister, don't think I can't reach you in prison. I'll be watching you. I'll make certain you never have friends, the same as you made certain I could never have friends. I'll destroy you like you destroyed me."

When I finished telling my story to this kind, caring stranger, I lay back, exhausted.

I had no idea how long I'd slept, but when I woke, it was dark and still. I felt damp and drained. A low choir of breathing hummed above the silence. I rolled over. Mitch lay in a cocoon of twisted sheets. A friend, an actual friend, in such a wretched place.

I stared into the endless depth of the ceiling.

Something wasn't right.

Fear, like a giant spider, crawled over me. Its eight dark, spindly legs encompassed me like a walking cage. The large body lowered itself down, smothering me. Fear like I had known too many times before.

I sensed her before I saw her. Impossible. Brigitte couldn't have gotten in. Yet there she stood, silhouetted in the partially open cell door. Raising a finger to her mouth, she moved towards Mitch's bed.

"No," I mumbled.

Without a sound, she walked up to Mitch's cot.

"Dearest sister, I warned you. I told you I could get to you. I said no friends. Now I'll have to take this one, too."

I sat up. "I won't let you. I'll stop you."

"Little Jeannie. You can never stop me. What do you think? Should I strangle your new friend or suffocate her with her pillow? How do you think she'd prefer to die?"

"I'll scream. The guards will come."

"By the time they get here, it'll be too late. Besides, they'll think you did it. No one believes you. You know that."

I leapt out of bed. "You won't get away with it. Not this time."

She reached down, her fingers starting to encase Mitch's exposed neck.

I tried to pull her back.

"It's no use, Jeannie. I'm too strong for you."

I strained at Brigitte's hands, trying to free Mitch's throat. A rasping sound escaped from her mouth. Brigitte's fingers tightened.

Mitch was awake now. She struggled. Her eyes bulged. She gasped. "Jean—nie."

Flo shrieked and cursed. Soon other voices joined in. Mitch kicked violently. She gagged.

I screamed, "Brigitte. Stop."

I pried at the vice around Mitch's neck, but her hold only got tighter. Lights flashed on around us. The place erupted with a cacophony of shouting. I pulled back on Brigitte's fingers using all my strength. Grunting from the effort, lips against her ear, I pushed the words out between gritted teeth. "They're coming, sister. I won't let you finish this time. This time they'll get you."

Brigitte turned her head; her eyes locked onto mine. Her grip stayed tight.

Mitch's face went taut. Her eyes glazed over.

I pulled harder at the hands clamped around Mitch's neck. "Brigitte, don't do this."

The latch clanged behind me. Heavy rapid footsteps echoed down the corridor. Fingers dug into my shoulders. They yanked me away from the bed.

"No, not me. Stop her. She's going to kill Mitch."

Arms encompassed my waist, hoisted me off the ground. I slammed onto the concrete floor. My breath shot from my searing chest. A heavy body landed on my back forcing a wail from my empty lungs. My hands were wrenched behind me. I winced as cold metal dug into my wrists.

Strong arms hoisted me back to my feet. Mitch lay motionless on the bed. A guard leaned down, her ear at Mitch's mouth and two fingers pressed against the side of her neck. "Call the paramedics. She's still breathing. Heartbeat's weak but there."

I swooned. "Thank God. She's alive."

My body spun around, a guard on each side. They propelled me to the door. I swung my head back and forth, frantic, searching the cell.

"Brigitte, where's Brigitte? You let her escape. Find her."

The guards pulled me into the hall. "Why the hell did you do it?" Shannon spit out. "You piece of shit. You almost killed her."

"What are you talking about? It was Brigitte. Not me."

I staggered forward, anger and hopelessness engulfing me. "Don't you understand? If I hadn't fought her, she would have succeeded. I beat Brigitte. I saved Mitch."

Shannon stopped in front of Flo's cell. Turning, she shook me so hard I couldn't focus.

"Are you fucking crazy?" Shannon's eyes blazed. "You and Mitch were the only two in that cell, and you almost killed her."

"No. It—it —it was Brigitte. She came back like she said she would. I…"

Shannon twisted my arm. I howled. Pain shot through my shoulder. I went limp. The two guards hauled me away, my feet dragging.

Then I heard it.

The great lie.

That's why they let Brigitte go. She had gotten to them first. They believed the lie.

Flo's voice followed me down the hall. "I warned Mitch she was a nut case. I read about the trial in the local rag."

"Does she even have a sister?" hissed another inmate.

"Yeah, her twin sister Brigitte, just like she said. But not regular twins. They were born Siamese. You know, stuck together. The doctors tried to cut 'em apart. Jeannie lived. The one called Brigitte died. Not enough organs or somethin'. Hell, Brigitte's been dead for twenty-five years."

THE SALESMAN

"He parted the low canopy of leaves. There it hung, a woman's wristwatch suspended from a branch by its open clasp.

THE SALESMAN

The afternoon heat pressed Hank's body like a vice. He wiped the perspiration from his forehead and frowned at the resulting stain on his white cuff. If he didn't close a sale soon, he wouldn't even be able to afford dry-cleaning.

A green oasis a short distance down the side street caught his attention. A sign pointed the way, its white letters stating Burnside Park. He glanced ahead at his car baking under the cloudless sky, and then back at the treed park. Where was he rushing to anyway? Another doctor with no time to see him? Another wait in a reception room with crying babies and exhausted mothers, where the only positive thing was the air conditioning?

He smiled for the first time that day. Hell, a few minutes communing with nature might do him some good, maybe bring back some of that old spark that had made him the number one salesman for three years running…1984 to 1986.

Five years and a lifetime ago.

That was back before he got slammed for enhancing his sales figures. Shit, it wasn't like he was the only one doing it.

Back before Jennifer left him. When the going got tough, the wife got going. The emptiness returned.

Back before he'd gotten so ticked off with an obnoxious client that he smashed a window and launched his computer terminal into the stratosphere. He could still see it hurtling down ten stories to its death. No real loss, the damn thing never worked right anyway.

He had spent six months in the penalty box doing *anger management* with a shrink. The company took him back, all right—and stuck him with this crappy territory. There were days he wished he had flown out the window with his computer terminal.

He loosened his red polyester power tie and used it to rub the back of his broad neck. Here he was, reduced to driving a seven-year-old Volvo through the back roads of America, sleeping in cheap hotels and eating too much day-old fried chicken from a cooler in his trunk.

Hank entered the park through its stately wrought-iron gates. The relief of shade welcomed him. As his discomfort lessened, so did his irritation level. It wasn't as if he hadn't made his own decisions. At least the company, unlike Jennifer, had given him a second chance. His breath came more freely. The air even smelled cooler.

He turned up a small path and, after a few minutes, plopped his sweaty five-foot-eleven frame on a bench and closed his eyes. A squirrel chattered somewhere behind him.

Twenty minutes must have floated by before consciousness crept back. It took another five or more to force his eyelids open. When he stood to go, something glistened from across the way. He sat back down. Whatever it was flashed at him again. Hank rose and inched across the path as if trying to keep an elusive lighthouse in sight. When he reached the far side, the beacon disappeared.

What he wouldn't do to avoid his next appointment. Even a discarded candy wrapper or a beer can provided an excuse to procrastinate. He started back down the path but saw it again, a brief burst of gold. Precision aside, he took three awkward strides into the thick shrubbery. He parted the low canopy of leaves. There it hung, a woman's wristwatch suspended from a branch by its open clasp.

Bending to grab it, his eyes widened. Below the watch, reaching up through dense leaves, were slender fingers.

Hank jumped backwards, his legs almost buckling. His lungs held his breath captive. His head swung around searching for someone to call out to.

His body wanted to run, but his brain fought the urge to flee. He needed to see more. He needed to make sure he wasn't seeing things. He stepped toward the outstretched hand and leaned forward, gingerly separating branches and leaves. His gaze met the pained stare of a woman, her ashen face twisted with terror and locked in death, her eyes open and penetrating. Deep purple and red bruises marred her neck.

She held Hank hostage with her stare.

There was no sound, couldn't be. Yet the woman called out to him, spoke to him, pleaded with him to do the impossible. To bring her back to life, save her from the horror.

A mix of emotions unlike he had ever known welled up within him — a confusion of anger, pity, repulsion, and shock. He felt her anguish with every tear that wet his cheek. One of them landed on her forehead. A switch clicked inside his brain. Panic struck. His pulse accelerated. He turned and bolted down the path.

He stopped in confusion at the iron gates, bent over, panting. A stream of sweat ran down his sides and chest. Muscles froze with the realization that he was no longer alone.

An elderly woman tottered by.

Tires squealed to his left. A police car sped towards him.

Another dose of adrenaline pumped into his veins. His bladder threatened to explode.

He straightened up as the patrol car raced by. The old lady didn't give him any notice.

Only then, looking down at his hands, did he realize he clutched the dead woman's watch.

He almost lost hold of the fine gold links as his fingers tripped over themselves. The watch flipped into his other hand. Engraved on the back was an inscription. Hank held it up. Squinted. *To Dayna, love Barry*. Her name was Dayna—had been Dayna. My God, what was he going to do? He had her watch. They'd think he killed her. But, if he went back to replace it, he might be seen.

***

The precinct office was unusually quiet. Detective Grant Fisher was using the time to chip away at the mountain of paperwork on his desk when Constable Dennis Turner entered.

"Sorry to interrupt, sir, but it's almost five o'clock. You said…"

"Already? Damn!" Detective Fisher bolted to his feet. "I promised Rebecca I wouldn't be late for her first pitch." He grabbed his hat from the rack. "If anything urgent comes up, page me. On second thought, just handle it." Stepping around Dennis, he rushed into the hall.

"Sir, the garage called. Your car isn't ready yet. I booked a patrol car for you. It's parked at the front door. Jim can give you the keys on your way out."

Fisher sped out of the compound. Turning onto Dorrel Avenue, he caught sight of someone jogging through the Burnside Park gates. His intuition told him there was something incongruous about a middle-aged, overweight man in a suit jogging in eighty-degree weather. But the clock on his dashboard told him he only had five minutes to get to the high school bleachers. He stomped on the gas pedal and accelerated.

***

Standing outside the park gates, a painful side stitch developing below his belt, Hank decided his only option was to pretend he hadn't seen anything. He'd keep his evening appointments, keep his motel reservation, and drive to the next town in the morning, where he could get rid of the watch. Eventually, she would be found by someone else. It didn't need to be him. After all, she was dead. There wasn't anything he could do to help her.

On the other hand, if he went to the police, a salesman passing through town, a history of angry outbursts, a single man handing over the watch of a murdered woman, what then? The police would be negligent if they didn't consider him a suspect.

No, it was far better not to get involved. He couldn't help the police, and he certainly couldn't help her…Dayna. Still hurting, he hastened up the street, his lungs heaving all the way to his car.

By the time Hank finished his appointments, the heat had begun to subside. Sitting in his car with the air conditioning blasting, he struggled through a submarine sandwich, tasting nothing, while his mind replayed images from the park. He took the woman's watch out of the glove compartment and laid it on the seat beside him. In its crystal face, he imagined her living face, a cheerful expression in her blue-grey eyes, pleasant lips, and naturally blushed cheeks, all set against a creamy complexion.

Why would anyone do this to her?

Someone must be missing her: a husband, children, sisters.

Was she married? Hank hadn't noticed a ring, but then, it was her right hand reaching up for the watch, not her left. A realization struck him. The woman, Dayna, must have been right-handed. It felt good to know something personal about her.

Then he saw her dead face, pale and cold with an expression of fear chiselled in stone. This wasn't right. Dayna was a human being—had been a human being. Someone's daughter. Maybe someone's mother. She deserved better than this. His breathing got shallow. A shiver crept across his shoulders. His neck muscles tightened to the verge of cramping. He couldn't just leave her there. He threw the soggy sandwich wrapper into the back seat, drew in a deep breath and slammed the car into gear.

Dusk dulled the sky, the resulting shadows disappearing in their own length. Hank parked his Volvo directly in front of the gates. Surely, Dayna had been found by now. Certainly, the police would have been and gone, leaving yellow police tape blocking the path, and he could turn around and go on with his life. Still, he had to know. He walked a short distance up the path, hesitated, and proceeded in full stride, hands buried in his pockets, one clutching her watch.

There was no yellow tape. At the bench, he stepped off the path. Certain she would be gone, he parted the undergrowth. Dayna's distressed expression stared up at him. His pulse quickened. His chest tightened. He held his ground and took a closer look.

Her face appeared fuller. Was it possible her expression had softened now that he had returned? Hank pushed aside more branches, revealing an attractive beige suit. He crouched down beside her. It was as if she knew he would come back for her, as if she had waited for him. Unable to help himself, Hank reached out for her. It wasn't until he touched her cool forehead that he understood their common bond. Both of them were dead, she physically, he emotionally. Both of them had been alone. Now, they had each other. In that moment, he knew why he had come back. She had chosen him to uncover the meaning of her death, to find out who had done this to her and why. For him alone, she had waited.

He peered out through the trees and into the darkness. Knowing it was wrong, he wedged her stylish purse between his belt and his stomach and then hoisted her up. Half dragging, half carrying her, he made his way back to the car, her high heel shoes weaving tracks in the wood chips.

Hank parked parallel to the sidewalk, the passenger door directly in front of his motel room. He scanned the parking lot and the walkway in both directions. Only two other cars were in the lot, both in front of rooms at least six units from his. He unlocked the door to room109. Leaving his gold Cross pen wedged in the opening, the door remained ajar. Under the dim glow of the motel's garish neon sign, he slid an arm behind Dayna's shoulders, the other under her knees, and lifted her out of the car. Her body had an unnatural stiffness. An unpleasant odour rose over her floral perfume.

He considered placing her on his bed but decided against it. Instead, he carried her into the bathroom. He dropped to one knee and then the other, resting his elbows on the edge of the tub. As he lowered her into it, his elbow slipped forward. He toppled to the left, the porcelain side jamming into his underarm. Dayna slid from his forearms, hit the other side of the tub and fell against the bottom with a jolt.

Ignoring the pain spreading down his side and burrowing up into his shoulder, Hank teetered back onto his heels, trembling hands clasping his face. "I'm sorry, Dayna. I didn't mean to hurt you."

After a few deep breaths, his composure regained, he leaned forward to adjust her position so she lay fully on her back. His palms pressed down on her knees. They resisted. He decided not to fight the rigid muscles.

Returning to the bedroom, Hank turned the air conditioner from medium to cold and set the fan on high. Despite a rattled protest, its stream of stale air dropped in temperature.

It took three trips with his cooler to empty the ice machine in the service room. After adding a fourth load to the tub, sourced from the machine in the front office, he knelt down beside Dayna. Even though she was pale and lifeless, one could not miss the sophisticated beauty of her features. She wore a calmer look now. The terror was gone.

Taking her right hand in his, he kissed it softly, her skin cold against his lips. His heart ached. He tried to cope with the fear and pain she must have experienced.

"You can rest now, Dayna," he whispered. "I'll find out who did this to you."

To keep that promise, he would have to be thorough. He placed her left hand beside the right and examined her fingers. A white circle marked each ring finger. She had been wearing rings. No doubt one of them had been a wedding ring.

It was ten to nine when he started emptying her purse—a Gucci, very expensive. Sitting down with a pad of paper, he spread its contents across the table by the front curtains and started making notes. First, the driver's license. Dayna Waters, 163 Downsview Boulevard, Cerina, Texas. A birth certificate—born in Boston. Hank did the arithmetic. Thirty-five years old, six years his junior. A Bloomingdale's card. A Saks Fifth Avenue card. That likely meant shopping trips to New York. A platinum American Express. She was definitely wealthy. A debit card. No cash. If it had been a robbery, why hadn't her purse and watch been taken? The watch may have been dropped when the robber fled, but not the purse. Why kill someone for a couple of rings and some cash? It didn't wash.

He went back into the bathroom to scan Dayna for jewellery. She wore none. If there had been any, other than the rings, they must also have been taken. Bent over the body, he gingerly examined her, moving ice when required.

No torn clothing, no scratches or bruises except those around her neck. He couldn't see any signs of a struggle. He studied her manicured fingernails. Remembering the hundreds of police shows he had watched on television, he checked under each nail. They were immaculate.

He withdrew his hands, rubbed them together and blew on them for warmth. He focused his attention back on Dayna.

"Sorry, I have to do this, Dayna. I need to find out as much about you as I can."

He rolled her to one side and then the other, feeling his way into her pockets. Her body shifted in the ice like a mannequin. His stomach retched. He swallowed hard and stared at her.

"Please forgive me, Dayna." She seemed to understand. *She must know I'm only trying to help. Together we'll get through this.*

Nothing in her pockets but tissues.

He returned to the table and continued the inventory. Two lipsticks, both light red. A compact. Car keys, what looked like a house key, two smaller keys. Address book. He flipped through it. Mostly Mr. and Mrs.'s, some of them in other countries. A few women's names. He unfolded a couple of envelopes—bills.

Hank leaned back in his chair.

He felt he knew Dayna a little better now. She was attractive, well-groomed and wealthy—and had been brutally murdered. He had lost some people in his life but none so beautiful and none to such senseless violence. He brushed away a tear and returned to his notebook and wrote down his findings.

No signs of a struggle as far as he could tell. The murderer was probably someone familiar. That's what the papers always said. Most murders were committed by someone the victim knew. Hank rose, returned to the bathroom, and gave Dayna a longing look before closing the bathroom door. On his way out of the motel room, he stopped at the table, scooped her possessions back into her purse, and tucked it under his arm.

He planned the objective and questions of his call while driving. By nine-thirty, he was in a phone booth dialling the local police.

"Hello, excuse me. A friend of mine was supposed to show up several hours ago, and I'm getting worried," he said.

"Sorry, sir, we don't consider someone missing until twenty-four hours have passed."

Hank could tell the cop wanted to end the call. "Yes, I understand that. It's just that she's always very prompt, and this isn't normal. If I give you her name, could you tell me if you have any information on her? Maybe someone else reported her missing, or, heaven forbid, maybe she's been in an accident. It's just not like her to be so late."

"I'm not sure I can do anything for you, but I'll check the reports. What is the person's name, and can I have your name for the record, please?"

"Ah yes, certainly. I'm...Harvey Mitchell. My friend's name is Dayna Waters."

"You mean Mrs. Waters? Judge Waters' widow?'

Hank bristled at the sudden urgency in the man's voice. He improvised. "Ah...yes."

"Do you want me to send a car over to check on her?"

"No, that's not necessary. She said she was coming here straight from her appointment downtown. I'm sure I'm just overreacting. Can you check your reports, though?" Hank fought to keep his voice in control.

"I checked the call sheet while we were talking. I'm not allowed to give out any personal information; however, I can tell you there haven't been any personal injury vehicular accidents reported this evening."

"Thank goodness. She must just be delayed. I guess I'm over-reacting. I'm sorry to have bothered you."

This time it wasn't heat but fright that soaked his shirt with sweat. Selling pharmaceuticals to doctors was one thing. Selling a lie to the police was quite another. Still, he had accomplished his goal. His deductions had been right. She was wealthy, and one of her rings had been a wedding ring, and he now knew she was a widow. Did she have children? Were there maids in the house? He needed to find out.

Hank looked for Dayna's number in the telephone booth's phone book. His shoulders dropped. As he expected, no D. or B. Waters was listed.

He grinned, ran to the car and rummaged through her purse, looking for the bills.

"Yes!" He ripped open a phone bill and went back to the booth.

After six rings, an answering system cut in. Hank listened to a gentle voice. "Please leave your name and phone number. I'll get back to you as soon as I can." His heart sped up when he realized he was listening to her voice.

He hung up before the answering machine switched to record. He couldn't be certain, of course, but there didn't appear to be anyone else at home. Very possibly, she lived alone. He recalled how he'd felt her loneliness when they had first met.

He refocussed. What was it he had told the police officer? She was to meet him after her downtown appointment. He had been improvising, but maybe she did have an appointment — with the killer.

There was no appointment book in her purse. However, she might keep one at home. There was only one way to find out.

***

After treating his daughter to dinner, Grant Fisher entered the precinct office wearing the glow of a proud father. His daughter had pitched a no-hitter, and everyone in the building was about to hear the play-by-play.

A howl broke his mood of revelry. A base, primordial scream. He saw the prisoner, hands cuffed behind his back, spin to the left and smash his forehead into the temple of the arresting officer. With another howl, the prisoner kicked like a mule, driving the heel of his boot into the groin of a second officer, who doubled over in pain.

Grant sprang forward and leapt onto the prisoner's back.

The crazed man spun and bucked. It took the combined strength of two more cops to drag the animal to the floor. With one last screech, he threw up and passed out.

Wiping puke off his sleeve, Detective Fisher disengaged himself, then helped Dennis and PC Jim Harrison to their feet.

"Where the hell did you find this asshole?" Fisher shouted.

"Joyce and Pete nabbed him at an in-progress B&E," panted Dennis. "When they got there, he already had the stereo, cameras, booze and some smaller stuff in his car. He was talking gibberish when they arrested him, but he didn't resist. Joyce figured he was stoned on something."

"I think Joyce figured right," grunted Fisher. He smelled his sleeve, grimacing. "I need to wash up. Have you found the owners of the house?"

"Yes, they're on their way down to identify their belongings and make a statement. I'll handle it from here, sir," said Dennis.

Detective Fisher pushed open the washroom door, holding his vomit-stained jacket in front of him.

***

Dayna's sprawling, Spanish-styled bungalow sat on a brightly lit street lined with mature trees. The house was set back some fifty feet from the curb. An interlock driveway led to an attached, three-car garage on the west side of the house. Like its neighbours, it was encompassed by manicured lawns and perfect decorative bushes.

No one in this neighbourhood pushed their own lawnmowers. The scent of cut grass and late spring flowers drifted through his open window. He had always dreamed of living this lifestyle.

Hank's sales training kicked in the moment he left his car. Rule number one, confidence closes sales. He strode up the winding walk of number 163 like he owned it, inserted Dayna's key into the lock of one of the double doors, and let himself in.

From the spacious foyer, he followed a hall to an ultra-modern kitchen and let out a slow whistle. The granite countertops and stainless-steel appliances were quite a contrast to his galley kitchen with its twenty-four-inch range.

He continued down the hallway, to a bathroom. Across the hall was a seven-foot oak door. Behind it, a well-appointed office. A beautiful modern desk sat to one side of the room facing large windows looking out into the darkness. Across the room, two armchairs snuggled up to a gas fireplace, a mahogany coffee table between them. On the far right wall, a floor-to-ceiling unit displayed volumes of books, a miniature sound system, attractive ceramics, and a dry bar.

Hank poured a Jack Daniel's, tinkered with the sound system until some quiet music emerged, and retired to Dayna's oversized office chair.

"Ah, Dayna, here's to you. Thanks for sharing the good life, if only for a few minutes." He leaned back in the chair, enjoying the calming effect of the music and the alcohol.

His drink finished, Hank began his search. The top right drawer of Dayna's desk revealed a tidy collection of pens, clips and the like. The one below held neatly labeled, colour-coded files. The small drawer on the left was locked. He took out her keys. One of the small ones fit.

Inside the drawer lay a pistol with a mother-of-pearl handle. He inspected it with respect. It was loaded.

"Were you afraid of someone, Dayna?"

He replaced the gun.

In the middle drawer—jackpot—a leather-bound day planner.

The phone rang.

Hank considered his options.

It rang again.

There was risk involved, but he wasn't in a position to pass up any opportunity to obtain more information.

It rang a third time. He picked it up before the answering system clicked in.

"Waters' residence."

He heard breathing but no voice.

Hank said nothing.

"Is Dayna there?" a man asked.

"I'm sorry. She isn't in at the moment. Can I take a message?"

"Who is this?" The question was expected, but the voice was terse, almost annoyed.

"This, sir, is Harvey Mitchell. Who are you?" Simultaneously, Hank flipped the pages of Dayna's appointment book. His finger came to rest on June 14. There were several entries in ink: hairdresser at nine-thirty, lunch at Chez Louis with Miriam, Historical

Society meeting at one-thirty, and lastly, Donald, hastily penciled in for three-thirty. No location.

"I don't know a Harvey Mitchell," the voice responded.

"That doesn't surprise me," said Hank. "I normally associate with polite people. With whom do I have the pleasure of speaking?"

"I'm Donald Hamilton. Dayna has never mentioned your name, and I'm a close friend of hers." The voice was beginning to soften, but Hank tensed at the underlying emotion, not certain if it was suspicion or fear.

The caller continued. "I'm surprised I don't know you, Mr. Mitchell. Are you new on staff? You're working rather late."

Hank didn't have to fake his deep laugh. He knew Dayna would have seen the humour in the question.

"The staff? No, Mr. Hamilton. May I call you Donald? Not the staff. I'm her second cousin, now living in Canada, the black sheep of the family. No one talks about me much. However, Dayna and I have...kind of a bond between us. We don't see each other often, but when we do, it's like we were never apart." Hank decided to go for the assumptive close. "Well, Donald, although it appears she didn't make mention of me to you, she did tell me she was meeting you this afternoon."

Silence crawled across the telephone line.

Hank waited. In a sales call, whoever puts the price on the table first, loses.

Donald spoke first. "Yes, we had planned to see each other, but I'm afraid she never showed up."

"That's strange. She seemed quite eager to see you." Hank switched tactics. "She said something about meeting you at the park. Burnside. Wasn't that it?"

Again, the line went quiet.

When Donald answered, he confirmed what his silence had already revealed. "Yes, but I guess she got delayed."

Hank felt a rush. The secret of success in sales was to use questions and statements to draw out all relevant information in the shortest possible time. It had been Hank's strength, and now, with Dayna's inspiration, he was once again at his best. There was no question that Donald Hamilton was her three-thirty appointment and that the location was the park, not long before he had found her.

Hank considered the implications of this information. Was Donald telling the truth about Dayna not showing, or was he somehow involved? If he was involved in her death, he wouldn't call her house because he already knew she wasn't there; unless…he was trying to cover up his guilt by leaving a voicemail of concern, thus implying he didn't know she was dead.

Still, what were the odds that the only person to call her and know she was missing was her murderer? Not very high.

Hank left that thought, and Donald, hanging. He had at least qualified Donald as both a source of information and a suspect. As in any cold call, the next step was to secure an appointment in order to provide an opportunity to turn the "suspect" into a "prospect." The sales terminology was fitting.

"Are you still there?" asked Donald.

"Ah, yes. I was thinking about what you said, and I'm getting even more concerned than I was before you called." He decided to push the issue. "Maybe I should contact the police."

"The police? Why?"

Hank recognized stress when he heard it. "Dayna told me that after her historical society meeting, she was seeing you and then doing some errands. I was expecting her home quite some time ago. Now you call and tell me she didn't make your appointment. This isn't like her."

"No, it isn't," agreed Donald. "I'm a little worried too. Did you say you're staying at Dayna's?"

"I didn't say, but no, I'm staying at a hotel. We were to spend the evening together." Hank was amazed how easily the lies flowed.

"Why don't I come over, and we can wait together," said Donald.

Perfect. The appointment was set, and he didn't even have to suggest it.

"How long will it take you to get here?"

"Ten minutes, fifteen at most."

"Then why don't we give her a little more time? If you haven't heard from her or me, in an hour, call me here, and we'll decide what to do."

Hank stroked his chin. Donald certainly sounded nervous, especially when the police were mentioned. He admitted to being at the scene of the murder. He had, as the police called it, opportunity. He no doubt had the strength to strangle a woman, which would be confirmed when they met. The remaining question was whether or not he had a motive. Hank needed to squeeze in some research before Donald arrived.

His head tipped back for a moment of contemplation. Returning his focus to the address book, he flipped pages until he found a Miriam under "S", picked up the phone and punched in the number. Was Miriam Solbourne your morning appointment, Dayna? I'll soon know soon enough."

A woman answered after two rings.

"Could I speak to Miriam, please?"

"Speaking," came the singsong response.

"Miriam, my name is Harvey Mitchell. I'm an acquaintance of Dayna's. The reason I'm calling is that I'm a little worried. Dayna and I were supposed to get together this evening, but she hasn't shown up." He took a brief pause to let that sink in. "She told me the two of you were going out for lunch," a shorter pause, "after which she was attending a meeting of the historical society."

"Yes, that's true," said Miriam.

Hank continued. "After that, Dayna said she was going to meet someone called Donald. Since she'd mentioned your last name, I was able to find your number, but I don't have Donald's last name or his contact information. Would you have it?"

"Donald Hamilton?"

Hank picked up on the dramatic shift in her tone. "Yes, that's the one. I take it you don't think much of Mr. Hamilton."

"Donald Hamilton is a creep!" Miriam practically spit the name out. "He's so full of himself."

"Then why would she want to see him?"

"I have no idea. If she had told me, I would have talked her out of it."

"So, she did see you today?"

"Of course."

Time to create a sense of urgency. "Miriam, no one has seen Dayna since this afternoon. Do you think this

Donald is capable of hurting her?"

Miriam gasped. "My God! I don't know. He was all sweet to her in public when they were dating, but she told me he's extremely jealous. A few months ago, she said his behaviour was starting to scare her. Just after that, she had to wear sunglasses to hide a black eye. Dayna insisted that she'd had a bad fall, but I always wondered if he did it."

"Is she still going out with him?"

"No. Right after the accident...if that's what it was...she dropped him. I was certain Dayna was finally rid of the two-faced bastard, especially when she started seeing someone new a couple of months ago, someone she seems to really care for." Miriam's voice had raised in pitch and speed. "Do you think Donald hurt her? Should I call the police?"

Hank knew he had to regain control of the call. He mirrored the upbeat tone and slower pace of Miriam's voice when she'd first answered the phone.

"I'm sure everything is all right. I called the police earlier, and they said there were no reports and no reason to be concerned. I'll check back with them and call you if there's any sign of a problem. I know I'll feel like an idiot in the morning when I have to apologize for getting you upset over nothing."

Once Hank felt confident she had calmed down and wouldn't take the matter further, he ended the call. One thing was certain, take an insanely jealous and controlling man, add rejection to the pot, then blend in the arrival of a new boyfriend, and you've got motive.

Hank quickly left the house. He had little time to prepare, and he needed Dayna's help to do it.

Moving her was difficult. Soaked clothes loosened his grip. With considerable difficulty, he manoeuvred her into the front seat of his car, forced her knees to bend with the seat, and strapped her in.

God, she was a beautiful woman. His lips touched her forehead. He brushed away a tear. It was like his soul was torn and weeping. In some ways, he was closer to Dayna than he had ever been to anyone else. He touched her cold hand.

Driving with the fan on high and the windows open, the front of his shirt and pants, which had been uncomfortably wet after carrying Dayna to the car, were almost dry when he turned onto her driveway. Hank ran through the house, opened one of the garage doors, then parked his car in the garage.

He lugged Dayna to her office and tried propping her up in her chair, but she kept slipping off. He grimaced, cursed and looked around the room. He took some tape from the desk, and searched the house until he found a spool of string in a kitchen drawer.

After three attempts at securing her in a sitting position with her head slightly below the edge of her high-backed chair, he slowly drew his hands away. She remained upright, her hands resting comfortably in her lap. He turned the chair so she could look out the window while being hidden from anyone entering the room.

Hank found the switch for the outside patio lights. A colourful garden sprang from the darkness. He smiled. She would like that.

He fastened more string to the arm of her chair and let the spool play out, dropping it onto the seat of the closest armchair by the fireplace.

He turned off the answering machine, removed Dayna's pistol from her desk and replenished his glass of bourbon. Relaxing in the winged chair, he took comfort in the luxury of his surroundings and the joy of her company. The ceramic logs sprang ablaze with the touch of a remote control. He clicked the button again. The flames disappeared.

On the mahogany table beside him, Dayna's watch kept time.

Normally it was the customer who kept the salesman waiting. Not today. He let the phone ring four times before he answered.

Next step; Create interest and a sense of urgency.

"Donald, I haven't heard from Dayna yet. I'm afraid something terrible may have happened to her. I was just about to call you. Can you come right over?"

"Have you called the police?"

"No, I wanted to wait until you got here. I found some information you need to hear first. Let yourself in. I'll be in Dayna's office." He hung up.

He walked over to Dayna's chair and stared out the window with her.

"Did Donald do it?" He swirled his drink and took a sip. "I promised you I'd find out who did this, and I will. Donald definitely had the opportunity. He had motive. But I need proof. My plan is simple, Dayna. I'm the bait. If he killed you, he's going to have to kill me, too. I'm the only one who can link him to Burnside Park and your death."

He moved back to his chair by the fire, nursed his drink, and watched the flames.

The front door slammed shut about twelve minutes later. When the office door opened, so did Hank's adrenals. He took a deep, slow breath. The most important call of his career had begun.

A handsome man who appeared to be in his late thirties strode into the room. He had a full head of painstakingly styled hair and a precisely trimmed moustache. His dark sports jacket matched the tone of the lighter oxford shirt beneath it. His grey shoes were obviously new and expensive. He stood erect, one of those people who filled a room with his presence as soon as he entered. His lips were turned down in a frown, and his furrowed brow displayed concern. His hands hung at his side, fists clenched and knuckles white. "You must be Harvey Mitchell."

"Yes," Hank answered.

Dealing with doctors on a regular basis meant managing more than your normal quota of alpha dogs. Time to tip the balance. "Why did you call Dayna this evening? After all, the two of you had broken up."

The statement appeared to catch Donald off-guard. Hank struggled to keep his smile inside.

"I wanted to find out why she hadn't met me."

"I think you already knew."

"Look, I didn't come here to play games. What did you find out?"

"I found out she was afraid of you, that you were jealous of her spending time with anyone else, and that she had a new boyfriend." He paused. "In addition, I was told you belittled her. Far worse, you gave her a black eye."

"Where did you hear that?" Donald growled. He took a step towards Hank.

"It's interesting you don't deny it," Hank shot back, leaning forward. "I know more than you think. I know that Dayna was also at Burnside Park. I know she was attacked."

Hank pulled on the string with his left hand. The office chair turned smoothly. Dayna stared blankly at the two of them.

"My God!" Donald ran over to her. He touched her face, then whipped his hand back like his fingers had been seared by a hot element.

He spun towards Hank. "What have you done?"

His hand plunged into his open jacket.

Hank's world shifted into slow motion. He watched the gun coming out of Donald's jacket, and with it, his proof. The deal was closed.

Hank lifted Dayna's pistol. It spit its deadly contents toward Donald's chest. Twice. Three times.

Hank stared into the barrel of Donald's gun. It wavered and then fell.

A bewildered look crossed Donald's face. The dying man's gaze shifted from Hank to Dayna. He reached out towards her and collapsed. A red stain crept out from under his body.

Hank stood up.

He dropped Dayna's gun into his pocket. The weight of the last five years lifted from his shoulders.

He wheeled Dayna over to the warmth of the fireplace and settled into the chair next to her.

"I don't know why you waited in the park for me to come back, and I can't figure out how you knew I could find your killer. You put renewed purpose and meaning in my life." His eyes misted over. He emptied his glass. "If we had only met in the park a few hours earlier, but…shit happens, doesn't it, Dayna."

He leaned over and kissed her cold cheek. "Thank you for believing in me."

Hank took her gun from his pocket.

***

In the precinct office, Jim Harrison crosschecked all items retrieved in the earlier arrest. Some stolen items had been identified by the owners of the house where the perp was apprehended. A Sony digital camera and two bottles of Wild Turkey Kentucky Bourbon were claimed by a homeowner who had reported a burglary earlier that day. Two hundred and fifty dollars in cash was not recovered. That left a small but valuable collection of jewellery glittering and unclaimed on the property room table.

Dennis walked in with two coffees, put one in front of Jim, and picked up a diamond ring. He let out a whistle.

"Don't let my wife see this. I'd have to get a second mortgage to buy something this big. It has to be what, two, maybe three carats?" He put it back on the table. "Is this all that's left?"

"Yep, another diamond ring and a necklace with a locket on it," Jim replied. He picked up the locket, turning it this way and that. He wedged a well-chewed thumbnail into the edge and flipped it open. "Well, we have a picture. And there's an inscription. Why do people write stuff so small a normal human being can't read it?" After moving his glasses to the end of his nose, he squinted and cursed. "Damn, I hate bifocals. The doc said I'd get used to them but I still can't see a thing." The property room phone rang.

"I'll take it. Can you read what this inscription says?" He handed the locket to Dennis and picked up the phone.

Dennis held the locket up to the light. He looked at the tiny photo and then back at the inscription. "It can't be," he whispered.

Jim held the phone out for Dennis. "It's Pete. Says he needs to talk to you."

Dennis placed the necklace back on the table and raised the phone to his ear.

His body tensed like paralysis was setting in. "You're sure of this." … "oh no. It isn't fair. Life just isn't god-damn fair. How am I gonna tell him?"

"What's the problem?" Jim asked.

Dennis didn't answer. Instead, he slammed the phone onto the table, ran from the room and dashed down the hall. He burst into Grant Fisher's office, ashen and stuttering.

"Dennis, take a deep breath." Detective Fisher said. He waited for Dennis to regain control.

"Sir, you've got to get over to Dayna's house. Pete just called in. There's been a double-homicide-suicide.... One...one of the victims is Mrs. Waters." Dennis closed his eyes. "It sounds ugly. I'm so sorry, sir."

"Dayna...? Dayna?" Grant stood up. "It can't be. We're..."

He flew out of the office door, thrusting Dennis aside.

Dennis ran and stopped him. "Sir, this is going to be difficult. I know how close you two had become, and she got along so well with your daughter. I'll drive."

Grant tried to stop the stabbing pain twisting its way through his gut. His hands chilled. A pounding jackhammer revved up behind his temples. He ground his fists into his eyes. "No, I..." he sniffed. "Well...maybe it would be a good idea for you to drive."

Dennis led him down the hall. "Sir, there's something else. Remember that B&E earlier tonight? Most of the stolen items were identified by their owners, except some jewellery: two rings and a necklace. I didn't look closely at the necklace until now. "Sir, the locket had an inscription on it, 'To Dayna, Love, Grant'. It's the locket you gave her. The addict had Dayna's jewellery!"

THE ORDER

"The Order only binds us to exclusion."

The Order

Secrecy and Loyalty.

Jonas lived according to these twin virtues. He searched for even one reason why Salacia had violated them. It was ironically fitting and terrifying that he would have to remedy this situation.

"Step forward." His voice echoed in the stark hall.

Salacia did not move. "I have a new life outside the community."

"Salacia, The Order has ruled that you have broken our code."

"The Order only binds us to exclusion."

Jonas seethed. "The Order has announced your punishment. The Ritual will cleanse you."

"The Ritual only delivers pain. I will not participate."

Her voice, flat, emotionless, as if discussing a grocery list, triggered a warm flush on Jonas 'cheeks—a reaction he hoped the dim lighting would hide. He forced his clenched fingers to straighten. In his two years as Administrator of the Ritual of Cleansing, he had never been challenged. The possibility of applying the Force of Loyalty had never been a consideration. Yet, the questions spinning through his mind, eroding his confidence, weren't because of what he was confronting; they were because of whom he was confronting.

Jonas studied every feature of the face he knew so well, but was no longer able to see the woman behind it, a woman whose thoughts had once been as clear to him as his own.

His muscles and resolve tightened. He had a duty to perform.

"Prostrate and prepare yourself. Your mind will clear, and loyalty will return. Don't force me to take additional steps."

Salacia remained stolid.

His anger mounted and collided with his confusion. What would happen to him if he administered the Force of Loyalty against her, his estro-side?

"Do you live fully in loyalty to the Order?" Salacia countered.

Jonas roared. "Only the Administrator asks the questions."

"And so it is that I am asking. The Order has ordained us to be spiritual twins of the highest plane. According to the teachings, we have become one entity, currently separated in space but not in soul. Therefore, I can ask questions because I am you, as you are me. Answer me. Do you live fully in loyalty to The Order?"

His body stiffened as if carved from the same marble that lay under his feet. In contrast, his bowels were churning. His lips separated, then closed.

Salacia's voice hardened. "Do you believe and adhere to the teachings of The Order?"

His heart raced. He struggled to ignore the pulsing echo that throbbed against the left side of his neck.

Her voice softened. "You are a good man, Jonas, as I am a good woman. I know the teachings guide every aspect of your life. You are bound to the mandatory virtues: secrecy of and loyalty to The Order. Violating them is not an option for you. But I have changed. I now adhere to different values. I believe in freedom through honesty and openness, and I believe in peace through forgiveness. That is why I must leave."

"You cannot leave us," Jonas spat out.

"I already left."

"But they found you. They will find you, again."

"I let them find me. I came back not to suffer the Ritual of Cleansing, but to save your life and to ensure my freedom."

"My life? This is about you. I can't let you leave."

"You have no choice."

Jonas remained rigid, lips trembling, his mind working though all she had said.

"Listen to me, Jonas. Everything I know about The Order has been hidden far away from the community—

clandestine videos, audio recordings, copies of the spiritual teachings, strategies for isolation, details of the rituals, even names of the high senate members—with irrefutable proof. Everything.

"Within twelve hours, unless I am free to stop it, all of this will be electronically released for the outside world to see. You can imagine what this will do. Now that you know this, are you willing to violate the mandatory virtue of secrecy by letting this happen?"

Jonas hesitated. "If I maintain secrecy by allowing you to leave, but I don't administer the Ritual, then I will have broken my vows of loyalty to the Order. I will be soiled and will be punished either way."

Salacia gave the slightest smile. "That need not be the case. I have left you the path of cleansing."

"But you are refusing to be cleansed."

"To uphold secrecy, you must release me. To maintain loyalty, you will submit yourself to the Ritual of Cleansing in my place. Remember, we are one. Your cleansing is mine as mine is yours. The Order will accept that, even praise you for your sacrifice.

"You will then report that because I refused to submit myself to the Ritual of Cleansing, you sent me to the furnace and administered the Force of Loyalty, ensuring I would remain loyal and maintain secrecy for my eternity. Burn whatever you like, as long as there are ashes left behind. That will explain my absence, with no witness to prove otherwise. There will be no reason for them to search for me."

"I'd be lying," Jonas said.

Salacia nodded her head. "Yes, but the teachings of The Order are clear. Secrecy and loyalty above all else. Therefore, those two virtues take precedence over honesty."

His conflicting values squirmed like leeches in a bed of salt.

Her argument dripped through his consciousness. The soundness of her logic became clear. There was no alternative.

Sweating in fear, he stripped and lay prone on the cold floor, reciting the preparation chant. Feeling anything but prepared, he stood, turned and entered the Cleansing Room.

Salacia walked out of the hall, hoping to be out of earshot before Jonas' screams were amplified on loudspeakers throughout the community.

Today's secret would be theirs alone.

THE SAVIOURS

He sat on the edge of the riverbank under a large willow, his head resting against the rough bark.... The feathery canopy protected him from the sun and from peering eyes, though none were likely to be this deep in the woods.

The Saviours

Clay manoeuvred a pocketknife around the perimeter of a willow stick, the deft strokes a contrast to his large hands. A strip here, a nick there, a twist and a bore. He ran the simple instrument under his nose, inhaling its fresh aroma the way he had seen men test fine cigars. He touched it to his lips but didn't dare test its sound. One day.... One day, when he was truly free, he would blow the whistle loudly and clearly. His freedom whistle. It tasted sweet against his salty tears.

He sat on the edge of the riverbank under a large willow, his head resting against the rough bark. The willow's laden boughs drooped, and like a child dipping her fingers into the water from a moving boat, its leaves skimmed the surface of the swollen river, sending out v-shaped ripples. The feathery canopy protected him from the sun and from peering eyes, though none were likely to be this deep in the woods. He eased his eyelids shut. Even after travelling without rest through two nights, sleep only came in patches during the day.

In forty-eight hours, he would cross the state border and look for a small red farmhouse, a station on the underground railroad. An underground railroad.

Imagine that! Was it like a giant mole burrowing its way as it went or a regular train screaming through the darkness?

Never before had he heard tell of tunnels where trains ran, but he now believed it to be true. There were people in that red farmhouse, white people, who would put him on that underground railroad, on a train that would take him north to the Yankees where he would be free.

Clay had laughed when his best friend, Jimmy, had told him about it. "White people, helpin 'a slave? You been into some o 'the master's hooch," Clay had said. But then, hidden in the shadows by the plantation house, he overheard his master and the sheriff talk about that same railroad, how it needed to be shut down before things got worse, how another slave had escaped. The sheriff was planning to get some men together to cross the state line and burn the place to the ground. It was that evening one week ago, creeping away from them on his hands and knees, that Clay decided to find that railway station before they did.

When he went back to ask Jimmy what else he knew about the underground railway, Clay wasn't laughing anymore.

***

The air inside the church smelled like spring, hot and thick with a slight scent of freshly cut hay mingled with pine, blossoms, and sweat. Georgina looked at the other parishioners while Reverend Smythe's words rang out. Perspiration rolled down Mr. Foreman's cheek. Widow Brighton fanned herself with short, refined strokes. Georgina had disliked Mrs. Brighton ever since she got caught sampling the widow's plums without permission. It wasn't enough for the widow to reprimand her; the old witch had told her father. He had applied the belt with authority. Georgina parted her lips, extending her tongue just enough to feel defiant but not far enough to be noticed.

Her mother's corrective touch caused Georgina to face forward. The baskets were being sent around. Georgina fished a one-cent piece out of her lace purse and dropped it with purpose into the basket when it passed. She loved the feeling of contributing to the church her grandfather had built.

Her mother often told her that pride was a sin, but when Grandpa's name was brought up in school, she couldn't help but feel proud about being named after Grandpa George Tomkin. When history lessons were taught, he was mentioned more than once for the work he had done in establishing the town and opening the land for himself and others.

Her favourite story was one her mother told every Thanksgiving about when she was a little girl. A disastrous storm had hit their tiny community, knocking down barns and houses and leaving several of the settlers injured. When the storm subsided, the one building left undamaged was their little white church.

The only bridge linking them to the East had been swept away by the flooding river. It was by picturing his family standing on the shore with Jesus, urging him on, that Grandad found the strength to swim against the strong current and make it across.

The water had begun to recede by the time he returned with several men including a doctor, plus the tools and ropes needed to construct a makeshift raft. Grandad was credited with saving many lives.

Her grandfather had given the first sermon after the storm. He told the congregation that God spared their church because of the parishioners 'love for their fellow man.

The recessional hymn began. Georgina followed her mother down the aisle. As she passed the second last pew, she caught a mischievous wink from Tom Simmons.

At seventeen, Tom was one year older than her. From splashing in the river as small children, to passing test answers to each other in school, to kissing in the barn just to see what it felt like, they had grown up together. Tom was constantly into one form of trouble or another. When that happened, Georgina was usually at his side.

His wink and crooked smile told her he had another one of his adventures planned.

Georgina walked out onto the lawn, politely acknowledging the greetings of several adults who milled around chatting in groups. Only a few people headed towards the carriages and wagons which stood to the right of the church just off the road. While her parents conversed with the Reverend and the Browns, she sidled towards the left wall of the church and ducked around the corner. Tom was waiting.

"So, Master Tom, do you have something to add to the Sunday sermon?"

"What makes you think that?"

Georgina grinned.

Tom brushed his bangs from his forehead. "I do have an idea for some fun. We could take a ride on Harry's new horse. Did you see he rode it to church, even though his family came in their wagon?"

"Yes, I saw it, and I saw how it pranced and tossed its head. That stallion is as stuck-up as Harry."

Tom sniffed. "He just brought it to show off. Ever since his father was made mayor, he acts as if he's royalty."

Georgina swaggered around Tom with her index finger propping her nose high in the air. "Harry would never let mere commoners like us ride his horse." She dismissed Tom with a haughty wave.

"I wasn't planning on asking."

Georgina froze. "You can't just take it. You know what they do to horse thieves."

"I'm not stealing it, just moving it. We could tie it up inside the forest. Think of Harry's reaction when he comes to the back of the church and can't find his horse." Tom smirked, his eyes ablaze with mischief. "He'll go crazy. Of course, he'll see it inside the woods within a few minutes, but won't those be a fantastic couple of minutes?"

They crept hand in hand to the back of the church. Over a dozen horses stood tethered to the wooden rails, their tails swishing flies.

The stallion pawed the ground as Tom approached. Georgina's eyes widened. She took in every inch of the deep-chestnut horse, its muscular thighs, ebony mane and proud head. She glanced over her right shoulder and then her left.

Tom pushed another horse aside and moved up to the post. "Do you want to ride it?"

"In a Sunday dress? No."

"I don't mean really ride it. Just sit in the saddle while I lead it into the woods…or are you too prissy?"

Georgina stood straight. "I can ride as well as any man."

"Well, now's your chance to prove it."

Georgina moved forward, running her fingertips along the fine leather saddle. The stallion had to be sixteen hands high, taller than any horse she had ever ridden. She stroked its neck, considered the challenge of riding in a a dress, and decided against following her better judgement.

"Help me up. The queen is ready to tour the guards."

Georgina balanced on her toes, grabbing the saddle horn with her outstretched hands.

Tom bent down, interweaving his fingers. "Put your foot in my hands. I'll hoist you up."

She lifted her left foot, positioning it in his cupped hands, tested her weight and frowned. "Keep your eyes looking down where they don't see nothing they aren't supposed to see, Master Simmons."

Knees bent and staring at the ground, Tom nodded. "I'll lift on three…. One, two and up."

Georgina pushed off with her right foot while adjusting her grip and pulled hard on the horn.

Tom grunted. He managed to lift her an extra foot.

Level with the horse's back, she swung her right leg over its hindquarters, landing a little lopsided. The horse shifted, its sinewy legs stepping high, hooves pounding the ground. She clung to the horn and wiggled herself to the rear of the saddle. Manoeuvring her right leg back over the horse's mane, she sat side-saddle facing Tom. When she stopped shifting her weight, the animal's heaving sides settled.

Tom looked up and laughed. "I thought you could ride as well as any man. You'd be an awful funny man riding like that."

"Fine. I can outride you any day, Thomas Simmons." She raised her dress, revealing her petticoats, leered at Tom, leaned back and swung her right leg over the horse's neck. The horse did another jig. Georgina adjusted her weight squarely in the saddle. Back straight, she set her Sunday shoes into the stirrups, pointing their polished toes up and in. "Lead the way, page."

Tom slipped the reins off the bar. He grabbed the bridle and backed the horse up. Pressing his shoulder into the black and white rump of the roan beside him to make room, he turned the stallion around.

Georgina waved to invisible crowds that lined her route, glancing nervously toward the carriages as they walked across the small clearing to the woods. The stallion stepped high, shaking its mane and tugging back on the reins. A short way into the forest, Tom looped the reins around a branch of a pine tree. He moved to help Georgina down, but the horse reared and pulled back. Its muscular haunches veered to the side, butting Tom to the ground. The stallion bucked and kicked its hind legs, grazing Tom as he attempted to scramble out of the way, sending him rolling into some underbrush. Georgina grabbed the mane to balance herself.

The horse shook its head, reared, and shook again. The reins slipped from the pine tree. Sensing its freedom, it gave one final upright jolt and sprang into the forest, trying to brush Georgina off against a tree trunk as it passed. She clamped her calves against the horse's belly and entwined her fingers in the coarse mane. The stallion galloped into the forest, veering one way and then dashing the other, trying to toss her. Georgina screamed as the branches ripped through her dress and raked her back.

She stole a glance over her shoulder. Through a cloud of flying dirt and pine needles, she saw Tom clasp his hands to his head. He yelled something, spun around, and ran back towards the church.

Georgina turned forward, burying her face in the horse's mane as a large bough flew past, inches above their heads.

***

Clay peered out from his veil of leaves. Something sounding like Satan himself was charging through the forest, clearing a path of destruction as it went. Devil or not, it was headed in his direction.

He heard screams, shrill girl screams.

His eyes opened wide. A magnificent horse streaked through the shadowy underbrush like black lightening. On its back was a girl, looking more like a frightened angel than the fallen one, branches striking her sides and face and pulling at her golden hair.

The horse narrowly missed a large oak, bolting straight for the muddy riverbank. Clay grimaced. At the last minute, the horse locked its front legs into rigid poles, drove its hooves into the muck and launched the angel over its head. She somersaulted and landed with an explosion of white crinoline and foam fifteen feet from shore.

Clay watched the girl surface, sputtering and coughing. She thrashed towards the river bank, but the current worked against her, whisking her downstream. Her head submerged and resurfaced. It looked like she could swim, a skill he had never learned, but something kept dragging her down. She took several strokes. Disappeared. Bobbed back up ten feet further downstream.

To leave his hiding spot was dangerous, but not helping meant watching her drown. Clay took out his knife and sliced off a large piece of his willow curtain. He ran along the riverbank, yelling at the girl. Her wide eyes settled on him, then submerged again.

He kept calling out so she'd know where he was. About a hundred feet downstream, he judged he was far enough ahead of her. He lay flat on a tree trunk that teetered a foot over the roiling water, inching his way above its swirling surface. His legs and bare arms wrapped around the trunk like a second layer of bark.

"Grab the branch. Y'all see it? Reach up." He waved the branch back and forth, trying to get her attention. She sped towards him. He plunged it into the water. 2Reach up. Reach. Now."

Georgina stretched her arms above her head. The changing centre of gravity pushed her face below the surface. Her lungs stung. She forced her eyes open, trying not to breathe in the water that had filled her mouth. Foggy leaves danced in front of her eyes and brushed her hair. She could see her hands and the leaves blur together. A hard section hit her right hand. She wrapped her fingers around it with the same ferocity she'd used to grab the horse's mane. Her left hand joined her right. She jerked to a stop. Her body swung up, parallel to the surface. The water drove her body under the tree trunk. Her arms almost ripped from her shoulders. She gurgled a screech. The raging water pummelled her clenched eyes and mouth and tore at her feet. One shoe, then the other, were sucked into the river.

She struggled to lift her head partly out of the boiling froth. She gasped in a mixture of air and water. Her throat and lungs convulsed.

Her vision cleared enough to see a pair of large hands clamped onto her wrists. Her muscles came alive. She kicked her feet, helping her saviour move her towards the bank. As the water calmed in an eddy, her legs lowered. Toes touched bottom. With the strong hands still clamped onto hers, she squirmed along the side of the fallen tree trunk up onto dry ground.

Georgiana lay on her back, trembling in the tall grass. Ochre water spilled from the corner of her mouth. Her torn dress spread out around her like a dirty, soaked doily. A pair of brown eyes looked down on her, eyes that appeared as frightened as she felt. With effort, she propped herself up onto her elbows. She looked around. The stallion, visible a fair distance upstream, was ripping leaves off a sapling as if nothing had happened.

"You all right, Missy?" the black man asked.

"Yes, thank you." She coughed up more water. "Who are you?"

"I'd rather not say, Missy. If you're fine, I'll be on my way."

"Why are you out here alone?" She turned her head and spit out mud, some dribbling down her chin.

He wiped it away for her. Cleaned his finger on his wet pants. "You'll be fine now."

He disappeared into the forest.

Georgina brushed water and a piece of moss from her forehead. Her entire body shook. She sat up. Rubbed her arms. Held her stomach, trying to stop the uncontrolled vibrations spreading through her torso.

"Georgina."

She straightened, grew alert. Strained to hear.

"Georgina."

She twisted around.

There, by Harry's horse. Her father.

"Over here." Her voice sounded more like a croak than a scream. She coughed, spit out water and called out again.

His head swung side to side, searching. He started to walk in her general direction. Two men she didn't recognize moved up beside him, one being dragged forward by a pair of hounds. Mr. Brown puffed along a short distance behind.

She called out again.

Her father hesitated.

"Over here."

He met her stare and ran ahead of the others.

Dropping to his knees, he hugged her "Georgina, are you hurt? What were you thinking? What happened to you?"

"I'm sorry, Father." She sobbed, unable to look him in the face. "I only meant to sit on Harry's horse, not take it. It threw me into the river. I would have drowned but for the slave."

"A slave?" Her father looked around. "Where?"

"He ran into the forest." Georgina coughed. Water dribbled out her nose. She wiped it away.

The stranger with the rifle yanked a piece of rag from his pocket. He hung it in front of the hounds. "We'll find him."

The other stranger unclipped their leashes.

The dogs wove and darted, their noses skimming the earth. With a howl, they turned downstream, their owners in pursuit.

By the time the two men returned, her shaking had stopped. She had wrung out her heavy dress as best she could.

The dogs were back on their leashes, their tails wagging faster than Widow Brighton's fan. The rifle man led the slave, who had a rope tied around his neck.

Though his hands were bound in front of him, the slave walked erect. For a moment, his eyes locked on hers.

Georgina's father approached the men. "Thank you for helping us find her. It was God's grace that we met you and your man on the road when we did. Without your dogs, we may never have found her."

The one with the rifle took off his hat and wiped his brow with the back of his hand. "The dogs have no problem picking out the smell of a horse on the breeze, but it's a good thing she didn't end up too far away, or things might've ended differently." He looked at the slave. "Anyway, it turned out to our benefit. We've been tracking this runaway for the last day and a half. Lord knows what he might have done to the girl if we hadn't found them when we did."

Georgina saw her father shudder.

The stranger pointed his rifle towards the road. "Go with my partner, Jess, to the road. He can take the girl back in the wagon. I'll stay here and handle the runaway."

Mr. Brown nodded his approval.

They followed the stranger with the dogs through the thick forest to the main road. After he tied Harry's stallion to the back of the wagon, the stranger helped Georgina up onto the bench beside him. The dogs snuggled into each other behind the seat. The man was unshaven and smelled a bit, but his gentle manor made Georgina feel comfortable.

Her father mounted one of three horses tied to a tree by the road. "Rather than taking my daughter home, follow us back to our church. We need to take these horses to their owners, and I think a little public humility may benefit my daughter." He dug his heels into the chestnut's side and trotted away.

It wasn't the probable whipping that would come once they got home, but Mrs. Brighton's barbed comments and sneers that Georgina looked forward to the least.

The wagon wobbled down the rutted road. Georgina twisted the hem of her dress, watching a pool of water form below. "Sir, I do apologize. The bottom of your carriage is getting dreadfully wet."

"Never you mind, Miss. The sun'll do its work."

"Thank you for your help, sir, to go out of your way and all."

The driver turned his chipped-tooth smile towards her. "It's a pleasure, Miss."

"What will they do to him?" she asked.

"Who's that, Miss?"

"The slave."

"Can't say as I know. Can't say as I care. I did my job. I tracked him down. If he was mine, though, I'd use him to set an example for the rest. There's too much of this runaway talk goin' on, what with Lincoln runnin 'for the Presidency and all. If this keeps up, we won't be able to farm our land or feed our families."

Georgina stared into the forest.

"Sir, what makes men think they know better than God what their station in life is?"

"Can't say as I know that, either." The stranger clucked and shook the reins.

Georgina squirmed in her seat. A sweet, sharp whistle sounded from deep in the woods. She turned back. The single note sang out again. She opened her mouth to ask what it might be, but the sharp blast of a rifle checked her.

She sat forward on her seat, the first of her questions answered. Deep inside, she felt a pang of guilt, but couldn't grasp the reason. She hadn't done anything wrong.

The Unknown Civilian

"My mind drifts up into the clouds."

The Unknown Civilian

I used to go to school. My teachers told me I was advanced. That meant I read more and was smarter than most of my friends.

Now, I'm fourteen, and there is no school. Instead, I sit waiting. Very quietly.

The afternoon breeze tickles my neck with a leaf. Just like my sister used to do when she'd sneak up behind me with a long blade of grass. I brush it aside and shift my weight, trying to relieve to my cramped legs.

The brook sings to me and to every other creature in the forest. Even though they don't show themselves, I know I'm not alone. Voices chirp and scold from the canopy above. The ground is camouflage for animals burrowing and tunnelling, making a labyrinth in the soil.

The air is cool and fresh, carrying a mixed scent of new leaves and moist moss. It is a luxury that no longer drifts up the hillside into my hot village streets, now clogged with the rancid stink of diesel, dust and death.

A sound, not belonging to the forest, alerts me. A harsh, grinding mechanical sound. Squinting between the leaves that form the walls of my fort, I strain to see what's coming. A tractor—just a tractor—rumbling and clanking weary joints past me on the rutted road. I let it disappear around the corner.

Taking a deep breath, I close my eyes.

My dreams come during the day now. I don't know why. Maybe it's because I don't dream at night anymore, or maybe because my days are as dark as my nights.

My mind drifts up into the clouds. Taking fistfuls of white vapour, I mould tufts into forest creatures—gentle rabbits with curious twitching noses, squirrels alert and playful, timid mice sniffing and scratching for seeds. I set the tiny forms down, freeing them to run over their fluffy field of snow.

I tear off a large grey wad of cloud. Like grabbing a long balloon in the middle, I squeeze it in a stranglehold, forcing the material to bulge out above and below my grip. With one hand, I peck away at the top to forge a curved beak and strong eyes. Next, I pull wide dark wings from the round bottom. They flap and struggle to get away, making the fabrication of the tail and sharp claws difficult and dangerous.

My creation leaves me in awe of its power, power I can no longer control. I release the bird into the air and watch, helpless, as it circles and swoops, destroying my forest friends one by one until they're all gone.

With unjustified vengeance, its yellow eyes focus on me as it circles higher and higher above my head. I know what to expect. I've seen it all before, the power, the hate, the killing, the revenge. I rip away more cloud and begin to shape a rifle. I glance up. The bird breaks its flight. With wingtips stretched skyward, it plunges towards me. I rush to draw out the barrel, shape the stock, carve the trigger. The air above me whistles as the great bird grows larger by the second. I take careful aim.

Bullets! I haven't made bullets.

The fast-approaching talons shine like polished steel.

With the rifle held above my head, I prepare to deflect the knifelike claws.

The grinding sound of an engine engulfs me, shattering my daydream. I peer out of my leafy fortress. This is it. Now, they'll know pain. Their brothers and sisters and children will know the loss. My feet prickle from no circulation, a thousand needles dancing through them. I dare not flex a toe. My lungs hold my breath captive.

A troop carrier bounces over the bumpy road.

In slow motion, my fingers feel their way into my jacket pocket. A predator always moves slowly before it pounces on its prey. I know this, too. I used to watch the old tomcat work the fields; I watched young soldiers position themselves in the alleys.

I squeeze the deadly cold metal in my pocket.

The truck is getting closer. The hot air above the khaki hood shimmers. Flashes of sunlight bounce off the windshield.

I can see beyond the cab now. The back of the truck is open, a camouflage-patterned canvas pushed up to the front. There are soldiers. I guess a dozen are sitting in the rear, although I can make out just a few from here—their backs to me, rifles standing at attention between them, their hats shading them from the sun—my only witness.

I remove the pear-shaped weapon from my pocket. As if confirming a marriage vow, my finger slips into the metal ring.

The truck lumbers in front of me. The faces of the soldiers are now clear.

I pull out the ring and hold the lever.

One, for my brother,

Two, for my sisters,

Three, for my mother,

Four, for my father,

Five, for all the forest animals.

Now!

Standing up, I swing my arm back and throw with all I have left inside of me. I throw for my family and all the other dead families. The grenade leaves my fingers. It starts upward, turning end over end as it continues its journey. Then, it arcs down. Tumbling. Spinning. One of the soldiers sees it—or me. He's pointing. He jumps up. Others are turning. The grenade is almost there.

My throw is off. It hits the roof of the cab. I hear its dangerous kiss above the engine noise. It bounces into the back of the truck. The soldiers start to scramble, to tumble, to spin. The truck stops with a jolt, throwing the men off balance.

I turn and run, my numb feet unable to feel the ground.

I hear my revenge explode, loud, violent. The expanding embrace warms me.

More explosions. Not mine. Short, quick bursts.

My back vibrates. My head jerks back. Arms reach skyward. Eyes follow.

The cloud rifle appears in my outstretched hands. The great bird plummets towards me. Its piercing cry deafens me.

Crashing through the rifle, the claws rip into my back.

The force and pain propel me forward. My body quivers as if chilled.

My chest and face slap the ground.

My only witness shines above me.

Too heavy to hold open, my eyes close.

THE PERFORMER

…she watched Franz stroll back onto the stage, fit the violin under his chin and delicately, ever so delicately, begin to play. This was love, the pure, raw and often sorrowful passion of love.

Chapter 1

His music billowed through the cavernous concert hall. Each note hung in the air like a leaf in a tiny updraft waiting to be spun away by a northern gust of replacements. Hypnotic and soothing, it spread a cloak of peace over the audience, their collective emotional state almost sighing.

A field of frozen faces and limp smiles stared up at him, their eyes transfixed on the temporary sun of their universe, soaking up his energy. Franz babied the strings a little longer and then began stroking them with authority. The sound lifted, arced, and drove forward into the hall, building in pace and intensity with each vibration. Backs straightened. Toes twitched. Feet began to drum the floor. Certainly, this was unacceptable behaviour for such a concert, but then who had the power to avoid it, and who would ever blame them?

Franz had them in his grip. He elevated their spirits as one, carried them into the clouds, and set them gently on a rolling hill of some distant emerald pasture, thirsting for more. He thrust his bow skyward in triumph. Raven hair fell like a closing curtain over his face. He took his bow.

The audience stood and roared. And roared. And roared. *Bravo! Bravissimo! Encore! Encore!*

But there would not be an encore. Not tonight. Not ever. The audience knew this, but it didn't keep them from cheering, from trying, from hoping.

Franz strode off the stage, his Stradivarius clamped under his arm. He returned for his second bow and then took his leave. Five minutes passed before the applause subsided, and the crowd began to disperse down the aisles and out to waiting carriages.

Everyone, that was, except a young woman, a lamppost of a girl, plainly dressed in black with a red rose pinned to her dress and another to the side of her frayed hat. She stood in the standing-room-only section, silent and unmoving, as she had throughout the entire concert and ensuing applause.

It took fifteen minutes for the hall to empty.

Half an hour later, the cleaners had fulfilled their purpose and left. When the time came, as she knew it would, she watched Franz stroll back onto the stage, fit the violin under his chin and delicately, ever so delicately, begin to play.

If his previous performance had been gripping, if the concert had been mesmerizing, outwhat could be said of this private performance? It was divine. No, not enough. It was angelic. Still not adequate. The feelings it stirred were intense, intimate, consuming, breathtaking. This was love, the pure, raw and often sorrowful passion of love.

Nothing else could be said of it.

Marie-Fleuri suspected that she was the only one who had ever heard it. On a dreary and hazy night, she had stumbled through the back door of the concert hall looking for shelter.

Having uncharacteristically imbibed several pints of ale throughout the day, she had outmanoeuvred the unwanted advances of several customers and wound up staggering down an alley. Seeking a place of rest away from the mist that chilled what little flesh cloaked her bones, she had entered the first unlocked door she had found. She hadn't really known where she was, nor had she cared. It was dry, relatively warm, and there was the faintest thread of beautiful music wafting in the air.

She followed the sound through several dim halls until she found herself in the wings of a large stage, in the middle of which was a man—a bold, beautiful man in formal dress, obviously a gentleman. It was from him that the music came. Somehow, she knew it was from him rather than his instrument; the violin was simply the outlet.

She could have sworn her heart stopped. Paused, at least. When it started again, it felt as though it was outside her body, pressing inward with each beat. It rode the music this gentleman radiated.

From that night forward, she had followed him as best she could, asking a friend at one of the better inns to watch for notices of where he would play. She used what little money she had to visit nearby towns where he performed, always staying after the concert, crouched and hidden, waiting for the inevitable performance that began after the audience and staff had gone home, the one he performed for himself and, unknowingly, for her.

This time, however, she did not hide, because tonight the music had come home. Franz Stromeister had returned to London, to the same concert hall where she had first heard him.

***

Franz loved this hall. There was warmth in the acoustics that made the air richer than anywhere else he played. He walked onto the stage, barely paused to place his instrument under his chin, and then lost himself in his music. It wasn't that he didn't put his heart into the scheduled concert—he most certainly did—but what he played now was his soul. Each note originated from the sensual pleasure that was part of his being. This performance was sacred, and he shared it with no one. No one had ever been worthy. Not his fans, not his sponsors, and certainly not the critics.

The first piece came from his heart and was always created on the morning of the concert. The second he'd composed long ago for one who had left him in pain, taking his soul with her and leaving him this piece of music in its stead. It was the only tie that remained.

**

Marie-Fleuri knew what to expect. The private concert never varied. It consisted of two pieces; the first was different each time, the second, always the same. He would end with a deep bow and then exit the stage. She was careful not to reveal her presence, and never dared to applaud. The music was not for her to hear, or anyone else for that matter. She sensed this.

The magic of the first piece captivated her more than ever before. The liveliness of its tempo was sunnier than the others she had heard. The notes carried warmth, the effect relaxing her muscles like a fire in a nearby hearth. Thoughts and inhibitions slipped away.

When the second piece began, she allowed her guard to slip. She sacrificed herself to the music, doing something unplanned and unexpected, something that startled her surely as much as it must have startled him. She filled her lungs and sang. She didn't know the words, if there had ever been any written. Still, that didn't matter. She was intimate with the music's emotions.

Her voice rang out, saturating the hall with a luscious syrup of sound. She was taken aback by its quality, much richer than when she crooned in the beer halls, where drunken patrons, more interested in her bawdy lyrics than the range of her voice, would ogle her bosom and grab her buttocks each time she bent to serve them.

Feeling detached, she considered that it wasn't her efforts producing the sound but rather the gentleman's music being played through her. If she was a conduit, that was fine. She sang on.

***

Franz did not see her standing at the back of the theatre. He played from a sightless place inside himself. Even if he had looked out, he might have missed her—she was all but one with the darkness. When he began the second piece and heard the music returning to him in the form of a woman's voice—yes, it sounded so much like a woman's voice—he felt the acoustics must be playing tricks on him. Is this what Beethoven had heard after deafness robbed his ears of sound? Did he hear a symphony of women's flowing voices playing his creations? If so, it was no wonder Beethoven continued to compose and conduct.

Franz considered the possibility of an angel singing his sacred piece to him. But why? Was he going deaf like the master, or insane over his loss?

His playing grew stronger than ever, and the voice responded in kind. A wordless flow of glowing notes harmonizing with his. Perfection. He closed his eyes so his ears could focus on the majesty of the moment.

When the end came, he bowed deeply. Rising, he stared out from the stage. A woman stood in the shadows. He was puzzled. He was, to be sure, upset. Who was she…and how dare she? For several seconds, he held his tongue, for the words that would have ensued would have been unfitting for anyone but the devil to hear.

Not once did he associate the voice that had accompanied him only moments earlier with this intruder. Not once did he consider that someone could reach a level of mastery close to his own. Not once, until she spoke. Then he heard it. Buried but definitely present, a tonal quality he recognized. He wasn't deaf. Nor had the voice come from angels.

***

Marie-Fleuri dropped her eyes. Her face flushed with embarrassment. How could she have done it? How could she have been so rude? Surely, she had ruined future evenings of being energized by his playing.

"Sir, I apologize. I don' know wha' overcome me." That was all she could utter. With the suddenness of a punch, she sprang from her position and darted from the hall.

Calling for her to stop, Franz took a step forward, but the burgundy exit curtains had already closed behind her. He set his violin on the floor, jumped from the stage, ran up the aisle, and flung himself into the street. A couple of carriages clattered by. Two gentlemen in walking coats and top hats passed, locked in intense conversation.

The woman had vanished.

He returned for his violin before setting off on a systematic search of the immediate area.

***

When Marie-Fleuri came to the Friar's Purse, she ducked inside, slapped her way through the gauntlet of groping hands, and set to work behind the bar.

Chapter 2

Upon entering the near-empty clubroom of White's three quarters of an hour late, Franz found Sir Henry Godfrey in his usual corner, asleep. Two other lords were vacating their seats by the fireplace. Franz nudged Henry's shoulder. Eliciting no response, he gave the senior statesman a serious shake.

Sir Henry's eyelids flickered. He greeted Franz with a groggy smile and a clearing of his throat. "Ah, my good fellow. So, you've decided to join me for a final toast to the day. I had all but given up. A longer concert than usual?"

"No, but an unexpected ending, certainly."

"In what way?"

"I had the honour of accompanying an incredible artist."

"You? Playing second to another? I don't believe it."

"Believe it, friend. The woman I have been waiting for joined me in song this very evening."

Henry shook his head. The corners of his lips dropped. His cheeks reddened. "Impossible! I told you your endless dwelling on her was unhealthy. She's dead. You have to accept the reality of your tragedy."

"It wasn't Elzbeth, for Heaven's sake."

Henry's forehead tightened, his bushy eyebrows almost knitting together. "Well, who then?"

"I don't know. I didn't even know of her presence until I finished playing. I fell into the magnificence of her voice, not understanding, not seeing." Franz pressed his left hand against his chest. "She sang Elzbeth's song, not words but the soul, with a voice such as you have never heard. Nor will you likely hear unless you help me find her." His eyes dampened. "I lost her to the evening, as surely as I did Elzbeth, but this time I shall not leave her to the night."

"It is not my intent to offend you, old friend, but you are not being sensible. How could you have accompanied someone you didn't know was present, whom you did not see? And then you say you lost her? At risk of your ire, I must be direct. Have you returned to wallowing your grief in laudanum?"

Franz's eyes caught the light from the surrounding lamps like a magnifying glass focusing the sun's fire. "Absolutely not! That was a grievous error brought on by unfathomable loss. A temporary lapse of control, not to be repeated. I don't need opiates to leave this world and enter another. I have my music."

Franz lowered his shoulders. A slow whoosh escaped his lips. "Listen to me, Henry. When I heard her voice come to me from the darkness, I became part of a new world. When I stopped playing, she was there. Her flesh was of this Earth. Her voice, not so easily classified. I have played Elzbeth's lament for no one. How could this woman know it? More significantly, how could she know its source deep within my aching heart? She extracted my tears and then rained them back on me, just as the sun soaks up the oceans and gives them up as showers to be returned to the sea."

Franz slumped into the leather armchair opposite Sir Henry, resting the violin case on his lap. "Your question remains unanswered. It is the same that consumes me now. Who is she?"

A servant approached and deposited a single malt in front of each of them.

Henry lifted his glass. "A toast then. To the woman who dwells inside your music."

Franz tipped his, inhaling the smoky vapours. "Yes, you've said it better than I." He stood and drank. "I need your help to find her."

Henry stroked his chin. "I refused to entertain your morose longing for Elzbeth when she passed. I should refuse your request now. However, if this woman is alive in flesh as you say, and not just in mind, I shall assist you where I can but only until I determine the folly of your search."

"You are a good friend but unduly negative." Franz threw back his remaining scotch and stood. "Fetch your cape and cane. We start this very night."

"Now? It's late. I'm expected home."

"Then we have no time to waste. I have already searched the immediate area around the Theatre Royal. I was no more than three minutes behind her, yet…she was…." Franz 'voice cracked. "She was gone." His eyelids squeezed shut.

Henry leaned forward. "Sometimes, we need to accept what is."

Franz refocussed on his companion. "I will find her. The manner of her speech suggests she is from the East End within the sound of Bow Bells. A hansom can take us to St. Marie-le-Bow Church. From there, we will walk the streets in an orderly manner, first going south and then working our way east, which is not a direction I wish to travel alone. For that reason, I seek your company."

Sir Henry's eyebrows rose with the pitch of his voice. "But I don't even know what she looks like."

"That is not as important as knowing what she sounds like."

Barely audible, Sir Henry muttered under his breath. "Likely the same as every other Cockney.

Franz leered at his friend.

Sir Henry snorted. "If you are not back on laudanum, then maybe you need to be. You are not—"

"No time for that now." Franz picked up his violin case and marched to the oak doors, turned and stood waiting, impatience inscribed on his brow.

With a sigh of capitulation, Henry signalled the club valet for his hat, cape, and cane. He followed his friend outside.

From St. Marie-le-Bow Church, Franz led the way down Bow Lane's poorly lit cobbles, the nearly full moon offering more light than the sporadic street lamps. They went right on Watling and left onto Bread Street. At every door, he pressed his ears to the planking before pulling back with a puckered frown. He did not grant Henry any response when repeatedly questioned about his sanity.

They continued east on the north side of Cannon Street, passing poorly clad residents, some strolling, other leaning against walls, some sitting on steps, some wearing little more than rags.

Giving Henry a hand signal, Franz darted across the street and continued east, leaving Sir Henry struggling to keep up. At Queen's Crossing, the musician again paused, turned his eyes skyward as if seeking divine direction, then, head held high, crossed Queen Victoria.

With his sight fixed on which direction Franz took once across, Sir Henry strode forward onto the cobblestone street. A whip cracked. A man yelled.

Henry jerked his head left towards the sounds. Two black horses were almost upon him. With eyes bulging, mouth agape and his heart racing, Henry jumped back and stiffened, the pounding hooves and creaking carriage wheels passing inches from his toes.

After a pause and a deep breath, he ran across the street and caught a glimpse of Franz turning onto Great Trinity Lane. Within two minutes, breathing heavily, Sir Henry had closed the gap to a few yards. He followed Franz south down Garlick Hill, side-stepping animal and human excrement littering the narrow, dimly lit alley lined by dingy tenements.

Wrinkling his nose at the stench, he watched Franz move like a setter, dart and point, dart and point, sampling the air, not with his nose, but with his ears.

"Looking 'fer some company?" A woman stepped out from an alcove.

A man, a red scar from ear to chin, appeared behind her. "I can give yer two fer the price o 'one."

Without a word, Franz kept moving down the lane, Henry on his heals.

The young man's voiced followed. "Yer won 'find a be'er deal than tha 'anywhere."

The thickening mist, heavy with river water and tar, indicated that they were nearing the docks that edged the River Thames. Franz hesitated under a gas lamp, turned right and pranced along Upper Thames Street until he reached what was not much more than a slot between two brick walls. Muffled voices could be heard from beyond a globe of light hovering in the thickening fog about a hundred feet away.

Another dimmer glow was barely visible beyond that.

Breathing heavily, Sir Henry drew up to Franz and squinted into the opening. "You are not seriously considering venturing down there."

Without answering, Franz stepped into the gloom. The downtrodden lane was so narrow it appeared that his shoulders may brush the soot-stained walls.

Sir Henry stayed put, glancing up and down Upper Thames before turning to see Franz's tall frame dissolve into the murk. With a deep sigh, he stepped forward, catching up to Franz at the door of a dingy public house.

"Why have you stopped here?"

"She's inside," said Franz. "Can't you hear her?"

"No."

"Your ears are tuned only for politics, my friend. For once, listen for beauty. Above the ruckus is a songbird." He grinned as if ready to pounce.

"You can't be serious. In there?" exclaimed Sir Henry.

"Raw diamonds are found not with the jeweller but buried in the dirt. Don't expect this diamond to be any different. Come."

Sir Henry puffed out his chest. "Certainly not. What if we should be seen? No gentlemen of worth should enter such a place."

"Then you are truly safe, for there won't be any other gentlemen present to note your digression from respectability."

Franz opened the door and entered.

Henry hesitated, looked up and down the lane and slunk in behind his friend. For the second time that evening, he held his breath. The smell emanating from the unwashed patrons drew a marginal victory over that of spilt, stale ale. The intensity of male voices was equally strong. Rough, sinewy men and buzzing flies surrounded solid plank tables.

Henry and Franz stood among them like scarecrows whose black cloaks, hats, and starched collars hung on thin upright frames. Several men looked up, laughed, and whistled. A mug soared past Henry's left ear, leaving behind a spray of ale and a trail of laughter. The next flying mug showered Franz's hat.

Ignoring it all, Franz gave a slight wink and marched towards the bar. He leaned against it, stared into the barmaid's shocked eyes, and ordered a pint and a song.

The mug Marie-Fleuri had been filling clattered to the floor.

Franz reached across the bar and took her shaking hand in his. "If a pint of ale is too much to ask, I would settle for the song."

Her face registered the shock of someone witnessing a ghostly apparition. "Sir, ... I ' ...ow did...." Her frightened eyes paused at Sir Henry and then searched the room like a trapped rabbit seeking a rescuer.

The turmoil around them dropped from a roar to a murmur.

"Let me start you off." He hummed the opening notes of his tribute to Elzbeth.

Marie-Fleuri straightened. A shallow intake of breath. A squeak. She mouthed air.

Franz tapped out the rhythm on the bar with his open hand.

Her voice began to unwind like a thin ribbon.

The room silenced.

He coaxed her on, growing louder and more animated. He removed his violin from its case and played.

Marie-Fleuri's eyes darted to and fro. Franz lifted his bow off the strings and gently touched her chin, redirecting her attention. Her jaw trembled against his fingers.

Their eyes met. In that moment, Marie-Fleuri saw the world the way she sensed he must see it, a complex lens that transformed sound into a kaleidoscope of colours and recast those hues into mental musical notes. She followed his lead with renewed vigour, her voice strong and free.

Like wax drawn to a wick, awareness of her body melted into his music, a loss of self, and yet a soothing sense of wholeness. All that remained was her voice, drawn out by his playing. She had never felt such ecstasy.

Franz shifted his focus to the violin, nodding encouragement as the volume grew and her voice followed. Violin and voice, voice and violin, alternating in dominant musical positions like two performers in a play.

He turned, and together they faced their motley audience. Together, they proclaimed their musical union to all who would listen.

The crescendo. The close.

Marie-Fleuri started to waver. She grasped the bar for support.

Franz took a short bow.

Henry, a rivulet of ale running from his left sideburn, stood, mouth agape.

The patrons came to life in a cataclysm of whistles, taunts, and cheers.

Franz returned his violin to its case and passed it to Sir Henry. He circled the bar and took Marie-Fleuri's hands in his, speaking only loud enough for her and Henry to hear above the din.

"As inappropriate as it is for a gentleman to ask this, and even more so for a lady to agree under such circumstance, I must ask, for I have already lost one love. I cannot, I shall not, lose another."

Franz took her left hand in both of his, encasing it without pressure. "Will you consent to marry me, or at least provide me with a chance to prove my love and sincerity?"

Her eyes widened. She withdrew her hand.

He engulfed it again and carried it back towards him with a touch so light it may have been a feather resting in his palm.

"I have an honourable place for you to stay where we can spend our days planning our future. Until we are wed, the nights will be yours. I promise to be a gentleman in all regards."

Henry, leaning horizontally above the bar in order to catch every word, jolted upright. "Good God, man. This is a common girl. Look at her. She may have a superlative voice, but she is a barmaid. What will your followers say? What will your sponsors say?"

Franz 'forehead pinched in the middle. His head tilted as if struggling to understand. "She is not a common girl. This is the most uncommon woman I have ever met. Her birthright isn't in her name. Her birthright is in her soul." His voice raised. "My audience and sponsors be damned."

"Never say that of royalty!" Sir Henry chided.

Catcalls flew like arrows at the prospect a fight might be brewing.

Franz turned back to Marie-Fleuri, his voice again low.

Her face was ashen.

"I hope your silence isn't a negative response to my plea. What is your name?"

"Marie-Fleuri."

"Do you have a surname?"

"Certainly, Sir."

With nothing additional forthcoming, he asked, "What might it be?"

Marie-Flueri blushed. "Moore. It's Moore. Like a field, Sir, but only with an 'e'."

Franz smiled.

"Miss Moore, will you grant me the honour of becoming your husband? Will you be my betrothed?"

Marie-Fleuri's free hand vigorously wiped the countertop with a soggy rag.

"Mr. Stromeister, why would yer want me?"

Sir Henry looked at the ceiling. "Why, indeed?"

Franz 'eyes never left her. "Because you are the one I have waited for. Our souls know a connection that goes beyond this world. I know you divine it as well."

She scrubbed the same spot even faster. "I've only dared t 'meet yer in me dreams. Now 'ere yer stand right in fron 'of me an 'wan 'me t 'wed yer. If this be bu 'another dream then why no 'enjoy the par'y before mornin's bottle-ache breaks the joy. An 'if i 'be real, then may I live in a dream with yer." A smile crept from her lips and spread across her face. "Yes, Mr. Stromeister. I'll be yer bride. I'll be Mrs. Stromeister."

Franz bent and kissed her on the forehead.

Her body pulsed and flushed. Never had such a feeling of passion been lit within her. The heat spread to the tips of her fingers and through to her toes.

She very nearly floated while Franz guided her around the end of the bar.

The burly proprietor shuffled up and blocked their way, rubbing his palms up and down a stained apron.

"This 'ere's me 'ouse, mate. Yer ain 'takin' 'er anywhere. She's me bes 'wench and brings in more in one nigh 'than the other bitches do in a week, wha 'with 'er looks and 'er bawdy songs and banter. Yer can fe'ch 'er for yer entertainmen 'when she's good and done 'er work, and then you'll pay me fer the pleasure."

Franz pulled out his purse and threw a handful of coins on the bar. "This should compensate you for her bar services this evening. In regards to other acts of which you speak, I shall not pay for that which I have no intention of taking." He reached back into his purse and shouted. "This should be enough to buy a round for the house." Another fistful of coins bounced onto the oak top. Franz spread his arms out towards the crowded tables. "What do you say, gents? Should the friar let this lady off her tether for the night?"

The room erupted into cheers. The bartender glared and stepped aside, sweeping the coins into his filthy apron. Franz took Marie-Fleuri in his arms and waltzed her between the tables and out the of door. Outside, Franz stood trance-like, holding Marie-Fleuri's hand, breathing deeply as if smelling a rose rather than dank London air. "It's best we not linger. We will find a hansom to take us home."

"You don't know what you are doing," Henry exclaimed, walking away from the Friar's Purse. "Your career and your livelihood will be destroyed."

Franz kept his focus on Marie-Fleuri as they strode past the drunkards and prostitutes. "I understand your concern dear friend, but I believe I am enhancing both my career and my life.

"I shall not be able to see you tomorrow. My fiancée and I have wedding plans to discuss. I will arrange the marriage for a date as soon as possible, providing Marie-Fleuri does not withdraw her acceptance. On that point, I shall request your assistance. If you will do me the honour of being my witness, I'd be very pleased.

Our marriage, however, will not be made public until a time that I decide is appropriate."

"But the reading of banns will make it so."

"I will pay for a license from the church and thus forgo the need for banns. It is not uncommon within the gentry."

Franz moved forward, Marie-Fleuri at his side, stopped mid-stride and looked back to where Henry stood transfixed. "My fiancée will also need proper attire, several outfits including gowns and a riding ensemble. They must be of a fine quality and style befitting a lady. No one must know what is transpiring except for your dear wife. I trust her as much as I do you."

Marie-Fleuri placed her hand to her mouth. "Sir, I don't know 'ow to ride an 'orse."

"That is irrelevant. The point is, those who gossip will think you can."

Franz watched Sir Henry take in the fine features of Marie-Fleuri's face and the worn lines of her dress.

"I shall always stand by you, Franz, at your wedding and into the future, although I am not certain anyone else will. To accomplish your request, your fiancée will require the assistance of a good seamstress, one with a quiet tongue. I shall have Charlene send someone we trust. Still, rumours will spread. You will not be able to keep this liaison secret."

Franz tapped his clean-shaven chin. "You are correct. We must create an illusion." He looked up. "Offer nothing, but if asked, she is an old acquaintance who has come to visit. There was an accident, and her trunks and contents were damaged beyond use. Everything must be replaced. Of course, cost is not an issue for her."

"But whence has she travelled?"

"Tell them you don't know. Let them guess. It will provide the gossips with hours of speculation."

Franz patted Sir Henry on the back. "I will see you two days from now with our wedding details, the date of which will likely be one week from today. I don't wish to have Marie living as a spinster under my roof any longer than necessary. On Thursday, two weeks hence, I shall join you at the club for our regular dinner. You can then relate the fantasies we have launched this night."

He turned to Marie-Fleuri. "When addressing my servants, use a dignified accent, and for fun, add a dash of something foreign. With your range and control, that should not be difficult."

"Sir, 'ow kin I speak somethin 'I ain't 'eard?"

"Even better. You won't have a bias. I will instruct you on the way to our home. You have capabilities that I can hear, but you cannot yet appreciate."

Chapter 3

Marie-Fleuri said goodnight to Sir Henry, accepted Franz's hand and stepped down from the hansom. She followed him along the short brick walk to the steps of his house, gazing up at the three stories of stonework.

Once inside, they entered the drawing room. The furnishings, though certainly masculine, were better than any she had ever seen. Centred in front of a fireplace stood four large leather chairs and a low sturdy table.

"Would you care for a cup of tea, or would you prefer something stronger? A sherry, perhaps?" he asked.

"Tea, please, sir. It will help warm me." She trembled at his light touch on her shoulder.

"Not sir. Dear or darling, or an endearment of your choosing. Never sir." Franz lowered his head and touched his lips to her hand.

Her shoulders dropped. Tension dissolved. She eased away from him, watching his eyes shift back and forth between her and the hall as if he was afraid of being caught in the act. She removed his hand from her shoulder, but kept it nested in hers.

Franz straightened. "My domestic help does not live in the house except for Charles, my butler, who will have retired for the night. I shall fetch the tea myself." He walked to the doorway, smiled at her and left the room.

She examined her surroundings. Embers glowed in the grate. She stirred them with the poker, added more coal with the fireplace tongues and stepped closer to the rising flames. Seeing the black dust on her hands, she searched for a place to wipe them off. Finding nothing better, she settled for the backs of the fireplace gloves tucked behind the coal bin. She took quick glances towards the hall doors until the gloves were back in place. *Why didn't I see these before I fed the fire?* She held her palms to the light of the flames, blew on them and finished by wiping them on the sides of her dress close to the hem. Straightening, she noticed the mantel was clear except for an empty vase placed precisely in the middle, above which hung a portrait of an attractive woman. It was as if the woman was the flower that the vase was missing. With her fingers on the edge of the mantel, Marie-Fleuri drew herself up on her toes. In the dim light of the oil lamps, she couldn't be certain, but there appeared to be violins reflected in the woman's eyes. Her features were flawless, her clothes conservative. A violin-shaped pin held a lace collar around her neck. A matching brooch was pinned above her left breast.

A creak.

She turned with a start. A large piano stood in front of a bay window. One pane of the centre pair swayed inward, a result of the wind winding its way through a now open window. She walked over, closed the window and secured the latch. She ran an open hand over the piano's polished surface, chasing the dancing reflection of orange firelight. Her index finger pressed one of the ivory keys, releasing a soft ping. With a sway in her step, she continued to explore the circumference of the room.

In each of the four corners, ornate tables supported lamps and books. She approached the nearest, picked up a book, and traced the gold letters embossed on its leather cover. With some difficulty, the word Tempest stumbled off her tongue. She turned a few pages and returned the book to the table.

A variety of musical instruments intermixed with washed-out paintings of fox hunts hung on the opposite wall. Rather colourless and boring to look at, yet what the instruments might sound like lured her across the room for a closer look. After a few moments of contemplation, she returned to the fireplace to reexamine the intriguing portrait, again balancing upwards on her toes.

"I see you've met Elzbeth."

Marie-Fleuri spun around, reaching a hand back against the bricks for support. Guilt welled inside at the possibility she had violated his privacy.

Franz held out a cup. "I hope you take sugar. I took the liberty of adding some. If not, you can have mine." He glanced at a second cup already sitting on the table. "Elzbeth was my life and my inspiration. I made the unforgivable mistake of taking her love for granted. The night she left for her mother's, she said she would return if I agreed to honour our marriage ahead of my music." Marie-Fleuri's eyes traced a slow path across the painting. Franz' eyes turned to the floor. "Like a fool, I listened not to my heart, but to my bruised pride. I believed she would realize her folly and run back to me within the week." His gaze drifted upward and locked onto the portrait. "The next day—she ran to no one. She was dead, killed by some unknown filth who dragged her into some godforsaken alley and..."

Tears sat on his cheekbones. His head bowed.

Marie-Fleuri crept forward, took the cup from him and set it on the table next to his. "I'm sorry. I didn' mean t' pry."

He picked up his teacup but did not drink, his attention back on the painting. "These are things you must know if you are to know me. For five years, after every recital, I played a private concert to Elzbeth. No one has ever heard it before today, nor would I have allowed them to. The music you sang is her song, a ballade I wrote to her memory. How you could know the music and sing it back to me is a miracle."

Marie-Fleuri flinched. She turned away. "Then there be things yer must know of me as well. This weren' the firs' time I 'eard yer play 'er song. I lis'ened t' yer over a dozen times in the past three years. I came in one nigh' by accident whilst you was playin'. I was with drink, I was, but 'earin' you, I couldn' leave. Yer and yer music was in me 'ead all the time af'er tha'. I wen' t' every concert I could whenever I 'ad enough t' buy a ticket and the fare. When yer performance was over, I 'id at the back of the 'all, knowin' tha' yer was comin' back t' play more."

Franz's eyes widened. He took a sip. "Then there is no miracle. At least not in the sense I'd envisioned."

Marie-Fleuri shook her head. "I never should've done it. I didn' know." Her shoulders drooped. "I understand if yer no longer wan' me. I shouldn't 'ave...I mean, I should not have opened me, my mouth."

"Of course you should have. Otherwise, I would not have found you. Elzbeth's music chose you as it chose me. I've been given a second chance at love, and she taught me not to throw that away. I believe it is with Elzbeth's blessing that I can now let her go."

"Sir, I'm from Whitechapel. I won' be accepted in yer world. At bes', I'll embarrass yer...you. You 'ave, have books I can't read. You know people I don't know 'ow to talk to. I can only bring yer shame. Yer friend is righ'. 'Tis better I go!" She stepped back.

He raised his hands, palms up. His eyes moist. "No! Please. Stay. Sir Henry has legitimate concerns, but when I proposed to you, I did so in earnest. I shall not put you aside like I did Elzbeth, not for my pride, nor for social vanity, and certainly not because of those who believe themselves superior to you or me." He took both her hands. "Those who believe they are superior to you already see me in that same dim light even though they play a good game of disguising it in my presence. In this matter you are not alone." He moved his right hand and caressed her cheek.

The sensation stopped her retreat. Her neck and shoulders quivered. "Bu' 'ow will I survive their prejudice?"

"With me. Together. We shall find a way. Listen to yourself. With just one lesson in the carriage, you are already adjusting." His head made a slight shift from side to side. "No, I am not recanting my request for your hand. I pray that you will not change your answer."

He lifted her chin.

As soft as butterfly wings, his lips brushed hers. She wrapped her arms around him, pressing her face into his shoulder. His warmth took away the chill from her heart, but doubts lingered in her head.

His breath tickled her ear. His chest expanded against hers. "Then it is settled."

She relaxed in his arms.

He sighed. "Still, there is no need to create complications. Until the wedding, you will use one of the guest rooms. A lady's maid from another town will be engaged to reside here. She shall assist you as required and help you adjust."

She followed him up the stairs, her attention distracted by stark framed faces that peeked out from eerie shadows as Franz's lamp passed over them.

At the end of a hall, he stopped and held a door open for her. She hesitated before entering. Inside the room, the air was fresh since no fire had been set. The bed was enclosed by curtains.

He placed the lamp on the night table.

She tipped his head down and pressed her lips to his. He responded first with hesitation and then fervour. Her fingers traced a path inside his jacket across his chest. Her free hand took his and placed it on her breast. Her heart pounded. Passion ignited every nerve of her body.

A minute passed with no movement.

She felt him relax. He pulled away.

With a final squeeze, she let him go.

***

She woke, willing her eyes to stay shut. A dream? If so, she didn't want it to end. *Please let me go back to this fantasy and never wake.*

A knock and a male voice jarred her back to reality.

"Madam. It is past nine o'clock. The master has asked that I ensure you are well."

The master? Her eyes sprang open. A pale glow encased her. *Heaven?* She blinked, rubbed her eyes. She drew the sheer bed curtains aside. A rush of cold morning air met her bare skin.

"Miss Moore, are you well?"

She slid back under the sheets.

"Yes... Yes, I am... very well. Thank you. I been..." she forced a cough. "I mean, I slept excellently... and have just woken." She grimaced. *Does tha' really sound like a lady's accen'?*

The man's voice from the other side of the door continued. "As I was not expecting company there, was nothing prepared for your visit. I do apologize. A pitcher of heated water and a towel are outside your door. Tea and scones are waiting for you in the dining room. We do not have a lady's maid employed to assist you. I will be attending to that matter today."

"Don't ye...you worry." Her teeth clamped together. She placed a cupped hand over her ear to better hear her own voice, the way Franz had suggested. "The room, sir, is excellent, and I was quick to warm up once under m...my sheets. Thank you, uh, Charles, is it?"

"Yes, M'lady. There are also some parcels left for you by Sir Henry. From what he described, it was fortunate that you were not injured in the accident. A very nasty thing for a lady to experience, I'm sure."

"Thank you, Charles." She tried to refine her voice and use the accent Franz had demonstrated. "I shall bring them in shortly."

I 'ave t' remember t' ask Sir Henry what nature of accident I been in.

"I'll take your leave and attend to you in the dining room."

Listening to his footsteps fade down the stairs, Marie-Fleuri rolled her naked body out from under the sheets and blankets. She shivered. There wasn't a robe to wrap herself in. She poked her nose out of the door like a church mouse checking for the vicar's cat. One by one, she retrieved the towels, the pitcher, and Sir Henry's packages—four boxes in total.

She wrapped the towel around herself, feeling an unexpected, immediate degree of warmth. Exploring the fabric with her hands, she revelled in its touch.

"Wha' can this be? I' be softer than a cloud, an' so thick. For certain, tis not linen".

Emptying the water into the wash basin, the rising steam brought an additional blessing of warmth to her face. She sponged her body to chase the chill from her skin and snuggled back into the towel.

She opened the first package. A soft blue and silver dress fell onto the bed. Forgetting the cold, she let the towel drop, pulled the dress to her bare body and twirled like a princess at a ball. She tore at the second package, spilling out stockings and undergarments. She held them up one by one, turning them this way and that. She had never worn such things before. They looked extremely uncomfortable.

Chapter 4

Marie-Fleuri paced up and down the hall, each trip getting shorter. She stopped in front of Sir Henry.

"A week ago' I though 'I were dreamin'. Now 'ere I am abou 't 'marry a gentleman I've admired fer years. I don't believe the Queen could've been 'appier on 'er wedding day."

"Nor prettier."

She lifted the layers of fabric a few inches off the floor. "Are yer sure me dress is fine?"

"Yes. You look dazzling."

"I've never seen so much organdy and lace in me 'ole life, and 'ere I am sportin 'it. She raised a hand to the side of her head. 'Ow abou 'me 'air? I braided and pu ' i 'up meself. Yer wife made some changes."

"It's perfect."

"Lis'en to me talk like I've forgo'en everthin 'he taugh 'me."

Sir Henry gave her a light hug. "You'll be fine. The more I know you, the more impressed I am. Take a deep breath."

She did. Three times.

"Are you ready?"

Marie-Fleuri straightened and pressed her shoulders back. She took Sir Henry's arm. "Yes."

He rapped twice on the drawing room door with his cane.

A violin played Bach's Minuet in G Minor.

He opened the door and walked beside her to where Franz and the clergyman stood beside large displays of white and red roses, mauve violets. Marie-Fleuri slowed her pace three times in the short distance across the room, resisting the urge to run and embrace Franz.

He laid his violin on a table. His face reflected the joy that bubbled inside her.

When the time came, Marie-Fleuri removed her glove.

Franz positioned the ring in front of her finger. "You'll have to steady your hand if this is to join its partner."

She held her breath. The gold band slid up to rest against the emerald and diamond cluster she had previously only dared to wear in bed.

The clergyman completed the service. "In the eyes of God and your witnesses, may I present Mr. and Mrs. Stromeister. Go forward as one, in love and peace."

They embraced.

Once the clergyman had left, Sir Henry directed the couple to the dining room where a luncheon of pheasant, fruit, breads, and preserves was spread out before them. Fine floral china mingled with bouquets of roses. Rose petals adorned each serving dish.

Marie-Fleurie crept up to the table. "I've not seen so many roses in one place." She touched one of the white lace doilies the serving dishes rested on. "It's so charming. Thank you for arranging this, Charlene. You've made this day perfect."

"You're welcome, dear. You have Henry to thank for the luncheon and the flowers."

He laughed. "I gave Charlene a barrow of roses as well, just to keep me on her good side. I'm glad you like it."

Charlene remained standing. "Stop gloating, dear, and help me into my chair."

"This evening, I am both host and servant. Ah, the lengths I go to for you, Franz. Let's start with a toast to the new couple. May happiness always be yours."

He winked at Marie-Fleuri. "I must say, you have no idea what a predicament I was in before bringing Charlene to meet you. She wanted to know everything about the mystery woman staying with Franz, and why her presence must remain such a secret."

Marie-Fleuri swallowed hard. "Wha' ...What did you tell her?"

"Never have I lied to her. I have no art for it." Sir Henry took his wife's hand. She gave him a smile of encouragement. "Nor did I want to say much. I wanted her to formulate her own opinion of you once you had met. I said that you had attended his concerts outside London, that the two of you had met at one of his performances." He grinned. "I told her that Franz looked upon you as a goddess."

Franz tapped the rim of his glass. "Have you spoken about me behind my back?"

"Most certainly, though I've never said anything I haven't said to your face."

Marie-Fleuri's knife clanked onto her plate. "What's being said about me in the salons and on the streets?"

Colour blossomed on Charlene's cheeks. Henry's expression turned glum.

"Curiosity as to who you are is high. 'Why is he not presenting her in public? 'is the question on everyone's lips. I prefer not to say this, but I know you insist on hearing everything. Many assume you are..." Sir Henry's eyes avoided hers. "...a..."

Marie-Fleuri stiffened. "A fallen woman? A prostitute?"

"Yes…if it must be said so bluntly."

She bit her lip. "Franz, I may 'ave worked the public houses, but I made sure the blokes knew wha 'I was and wha 'I wasn'. I'd rather be thought of well in the ale 'alls of Limehouse than be called a whore in the concert 'alls of London."

Franz took her hand, his eyes sullen. "We will still the voices shortly."

"I pray you do so, soon." Her cheeks burning, she settled back into her chair and looked towards Sir Henry. "What else do they say?"

He squirmed and inspected his fingernails. "As one would expect, the servants have been whispering. They say you speak strangely, somewhat common but accented, possibly schooled in English somewhere abroad." He brightened. "But they say you are pleasant and courteous with genuine sincerity not often found in society. And all have mentioned that your beauty will be the envy of many. I have echoed those same sentiments."

"Thank you. Me...my heart takes some relief from that. Please excuse me for a few moments. I have lady matters to attend to."

Charlene rose. "I shall join you."

When left to themselves, Sir Henry shook his head, his expression glum. "My concerns are for Marie. Should you be found out, this union will not be accepted. I know you love her. And I have come to admire the person she is, but society is not so accepting."

"Henry, I am more joyous now than any time since Elzbeth left me. I shall not entertain such discussion during our celebration, nor in the future."

Sir Henry sank back in his chair. "Oh, come now, Franz. I may be a little too direct, but I speak only of reality. Society is watching. Even as I arrived this morning, four busybodies stood trying to catch a glimpse through the open door. Cruelty and isolation will follow revelations."

Franz looked up at the chandelier. "I must insist that you have faith. Not born here, I have suffered the sting of society's prejudices. I've learned how to play their game." He looked towards the door. "Quiet now. I hear our wives approaching."

Sir Henry rose and opened the door, performing a slight bow as the ladies passed. He followed them back to the table.

Franz stood. "Please join me in a toast." He held his crystal glass high. "To my beautiful bride and our eternal love."

The two men nodded in her direction and drank.

Marie-Fleuri brushed Franz's shoulder as she passed behind him. "Thank you, darling. And what have you two been talking about in our absence?"

"Your beauty, your kindness and my fortune at having you in my life." He helped her into her chair, assisting her in adjusting her full skirt as she sat. "I also banished Henry's cynicism regarding other people. Personally, I can't wait to hear what the gossips' wagging tongues will be spreading when he and I next meet at the club."

Sir Henry became animated. "I'm sure I'll have much more to tell you then. Certainly, the greatest wad of wagging flesh is attached to the countenance of Lady Simpson herself. No doubt you have not yet received an invitation to her reception." He leaned forward, beaming. His hands pressed against the tabletop. His voice dropped to a near whisper. "This is because she is beside herself with self-righteous worry. As the event is in your honour, if she issues the invitation to you alone, would you be offended and not attend?"

Franz tapped his glass against his bride's. "Offended? Not at all. I would bring my guest anyway and do so with my sponsors 'permission."

Her shoulders gave an involuntary twitch. Her attention turned to Sir Henry.

He chortled, his index finger tapping the table. "But, if the invitation is addressed to Mr. Stromeister and guest, you might actually bring your guest."

Marie-Fleuri looked back to Franz.

Franz nodded. "Then Lady Simpson would be correct."

"But the mere fact that her elite guest list includes a woman who resides without shame in a widower's home, would surely make her a target of gossip. She is petrified into non-action."

Marie-Fleuri frowned. Her eyes narrowed.

Franz walked around the table and slapped Sir Henry on the back. "Now you're getting into the spirit of the event." He rubbed his chin. "Inform her that I request the pleasure of bringing a guest to her reception."

Marie-Fleuri watched the impish look on Franz's face. She ensured that he saw the scowl on hers. "Is there a mean side of you tha 'I'm not aware of, tha ' instead of worryin 'about my reputation, you use it to torture this lady?"

Sir Henry jumped in. "Franz has never hurt a fly and never will. He does, however, like to play with people's vanity, for which there is no larger target than Lady Simpson. Franz assures us that he will protect your reputation and your relationship. I trust he shall."

Marie-Fleuri sat back, hiding the uncertainty that hovered in her stomach. "Then, I got to do likewise."

Franz returned to his chair and slid his fingers down her gloved arm. "My dear, even Lady Simpson will come to know you for the incredible soul you are."

She kissed his cheek. "I don't know 'ow yer words and touch can soothe me so. I pray tha 'yer righ'."

With the meal and claret finished, Charlene presented their remaining gift, a leather-bound book.

Marei-Fleuri took it in her hands and placed it with care on the table as if it were made of china. She passed her index finger under the embossed words and read. "Per-I-duh and Per-e...ju-dis." Blinking, she took Charlene's hand in hers. Thank you. I shall learn to read every word of it." She looked at Franz, and with a light voice added, "With a mysterious accent, of course."

***

Finally, alone in the house, Franz led Marie-Fleuri, still clutching her book, into their bedroom. A single red rose lay in the middle of the bed.

He took her in his arms. "This is the day I've longed for. We have our home to ourselves."

The book thumped to the floor.

She pressed against him. "I wan 'to be with you forever. Still, every night I 'ave some fear of wha 'the morrow may bring."

"In the morning, we begin rehearsing. We have less than three weeks to prepare our performance. On that Friday, we announce our love to the world. The streets of London will be abuzz. By evening's end, admiration for you will be as thick as honey."

She separated from him, the back of her legs stopped by the mattress. "Dearest Franz, if we wait until then to announce our marriage, will they believe it?"

He lowered her onto the bed and leaned over her.

She swung her legs onto the mattress and hoisted her dress above her knees. She wet her lips and met his.

He slid his mouth across her cheek and began kissing his way down her neck. "They will believe us..."

He undid her collar. His tongue moist on her shoulder.

"...and here's why."

She attacked the buttons on his shirt. "Shhh. The explanation can wait."

CHAPTER 5

By the third Friday after the wedding, Marie-Fleuri was near exhaustion, physically, mentally and emotionally. She was used to daily labour, but this was far more demanding. Rehearsing had begun daily, thirty minutes after breakfast and continuing after lunch. Franz 'drive to perfection was ceaseless—never cruel, never threatening yet always pressing for purer sound, perfect intonation, precise timing, and higher notes.

Charlene arrived each day at four o'clock for tea, after which she had provided lessons in etiquette, manners and managing staff. After dinner there were speech classes with Franz, then bed, glorious bed, where she became elevated to new emotional and physical heights with lovemaking that carried them into the night. Waves of shivers ran up and down her back from his lightest touch. In response, intertwining his lithe fingers with hers set his neck muscles visibly quivering. Through it all, they developed a bond beyond anything she had experienced or considered possible.

Each day, the cycle was repeated.

The stress on her body and mind was intense. Whenever her body told her she could go no further, when she felt that not another note could be forced past her lips, when she believed collapse was certain, tears would appear in Franz 'eyes as if they were hers. He would encircle her cheeks with his fingertips, then ease them down her neck and lower still onto her back until his arms embraced and supported her. She would surrender, melting into him and feeling every beat of his heart. He would match her breathing and lightly massage her back. Prickling sensations would radiate across her skin. Energy flowed from him into and through her limbs. Ardour returned. Lungs refilled to capacity.

And she would press on.

In his presence, she was strong, complete.

But now, sitting alone in front of her mirror, rain tapping on the window, she looked up and pleaded for the same level of confidence in her abilities that he had. Each day his compliments came with increased enthusiasm, whilst her creeping fears predicted their performance would turn into the worst of burlesque.

Yesterday, Franz insisted they do nothing but rest. Though welcomed, it left space to worry. With the concert only hours away, she checked her makeup, her hair and her gown, yet again. Thank God Charlene had come with her personal lady's maid to help her dress.

"Oh, Franz, wha 'if I forget everythin 'yer taugh ' me?"

In her reflection, behind light rouge and curls, she saw a frightened little girl standing alone on the gritty steps of an orphanage.

***

At long last, Marie-Fleuri lowered herself onto the forward-facing seat of the carriage. She settled and adjusted her dress. Franz sat beside her, resting a hand on hers.

With a jerk, accompanied by several whinnies and snorts from the horse, the carriage set off for the concert hall. Marie-Fleuri laid her head on Franz 'shoulder, listening to the tapping of rain that accompanied the dull clip-clop of horses 'hooves against granite setts. She touched her lips to his hair.

"Four weeks ago, I was enjoying my life, as simple as i 'was. I had no idea wha 'was to come. When you proposed, it was like a dream, one I feared would end in pain. For wha 'possible reason would a gentleman wan 'me? When the minister said we were one spirit…," She touched a finger to her lips. Inhaled. Lowered her hand and exhaled. "I thought they were nice words, but no more than that.

Now, I understand. I cannot imagine ever being apart from you. I am near collapse, yet floating without effort. I pray I shall not disappoint you."

His index finger pressed her lips. "Shhh. I will never be disappointed with you."

She closed her eyes and drifted into an uneasy slumber.

***

The carriage leaned and lurched. Marie-Fleuri bounced and clutched Franz 'arm.

He smiled. "It was just a rut. We are almost there. Are you nervous?"

She gave a slight nod. "What if they don't like my performance?"

"They will love you."

"Even if they don't boo me off the stage, surely they'll recognize me for what I am when I speak at the reception."

"I hope so, for you are one of the purest and kindest creatures that God has placed on this earth."

Gooseflesh crept up her arms beneath her long mauve gloves. She called upon the confidence she had felt at the end of their rehearsals. It wouldn't manifest itself.

"I want to believe you, Franz, but I'm so scared."

Franz took both her hands in his. "I understand. I do. Take a moment to inhale and exhale deeply as I taught you. Send the fear out with your breath. Replace it with pride."

She did as instructed.

He studied her face. "I assure you. When you sing, they will fall to their knees. When you speak, they will hang on your every word. When you so choose, your pronunciation and language are perfect. Choose that now. No one will doubt you." His lips touched hers. She squeezed his hands. They rode on in silence.

The carriage stopped at the back of the concert hall, where Sir Henry waited, umbrella in hand. He opened the door and signalled that it was clear. Franz jumped down and helped Marie-Fleuri out. He led her through the stage entrance to his private waiting room.

Upon receiving a knock on the closed door followed by: "Five minutes to curtain, sir. Five minutes.", Franz led Marie-Fleuri to the wings of the stage where Sir Henry was waiting with two chairs.

The concert hall filled. The orchestra tuned.

His name called, Franz strode out from the side curtains, leaving Marie-Fleuri with Sir Henry. She grasped her stomach and watched.

Franz's performance was brilliant, better than any she had heard. He thanked the orchestra and introduced his final piece, a solo. Past the curtain's edge, she watched the audience drift into a trance-like state. Not a cough or shuffle came from the seats.

***

Franz closed his eyes and stood frozen, letting the energy build. With a turn of his neck and a sweep of his bow, the strings came to life as if under a mystic spell. He lifted the audience out of their placid condition, gently at first and then with zeal. He sensed stirring in the loges and channelled their verve. He reached deeper within himself than ever before and thrust the augmented exuberance outward. After two forty-minute sets of perfection, in a crescendo of music and might, he thrust his bow, violin and final note towards the heavens.

An instant of stillness erupted into a cataclysm.

He bowed and left the stage.

The audience stood and cheered, calling for more. Franz returned for his second bow, and in typical form made his exit without an encore.

As the uproar began to wane, Franz did what he had never done before. He strolled back to centre stage.

The main floor became a source of whispers, pointing, shuffling and confusion.

Franz fitted his violin under his chin, adjusted one of the pegs and then lowered it to his side. The air stilled as if the audience had turned into stone.

A beautiful flowing mirage drifted in from stage right, taking her place next to the Maestro. The quiescence gave way to a communal gasp.

He bowed, and she curtseyed toward the Royal Box and then to the general audience.

Murmurs again rippled through the air.

The master took two steps back, leaving the woman to own centre stage.

There was a consolidated intake of breath.

Franz positioned his violin.

The spectators melted back into their seats like a wave flowing out from the stage.

Marie-Fleuri glanced at Franz. He gave a slight nod and began to play. She opened her mouth, and from it drifted a voice that rang true and strong. The luxuriousness of their entwined sound took her somewhat by surprise. The unity of their efforts struck her as ethereal. She concluded it was the concert hall that added more than their rehearsals had revealed. A quarter of the way through their first piece, she glanced at the royal box and saw the prince press a hand to his heart. Her chest tightened. She shifted her focus instead to a blur of faces in the far balcony. Head held high, she let Franz 'playing carry her forward. Instead of simply singing notes, she relaxed and sang in celebration of their love.

When their second piece—the ballade to Elzbeth—ended, an awe-inspired tranquility settled over the hall. Women dabbed their eyes, and gentlemen swallowed awkwardly. A single set of hands from the Royal Box set off the applause. The hall erupted in cheers and tears for several minutes before voices subsided, but the hum up one row and down the next was the same: Who was she? Where had she trained? Was she from the continent? Had someone not mentioned America? Such beauty could not have been hidden anywhere in England without discovery.

The building took much longer than usual to empty, but when the patrons did begin to exit, some left with unprecedented haste. These were the privileged few invited to the royal reception where Maestro Stromeister and guest were expected to be in attendance.

Chapter 6

Lord and Lady Simpson's ballroom sparkled with polished chandeliers and mirrors. Light danced across gilt and freshly painted walls. Servants hovered by food, ready to serve what they had spent days preparing. Rare pineapple decorated dessert trays.

When all arrivals had been announced and the ballroom filled, two guests remained noticeably absent.

Lady Simpson paced back and forth across the main entrance. Spotting Sir Henry, she rushed to the far side of the hall and pulled him away from his companions.

"Where are they? I know the Maestro doesn't enjoy these functions, but surely he would not disappoint the Prince and Princess."

"They will be here. Mr. Stromeister had some last-minute affairs to address. I believe I informed you of that yesterday."

Lady Simpson looked this way and that as if expecting to see Franz and his guest appear from nowhere. "You must tell me. The woman who resides with him, surely she is the vocalist."

Sir Henry said nothing.

Her hands pushed her cheeks together, moulding her lips into those of a fish, then popped apart as if launched by springs. "It would explain the secrecy. But why allow her to stay under his roof without servants?" She picked at the fingertips of her gloves "I understand artists are less inclined to follow social protocol, and he is a foreigner by birth. Still, this is most unnatural. Please assure me there will be no unpleasant surprises when they arrive."

Sir Henry pursed his lips. He leaned in, almost touching her ear. "I assure you, they will be present. I also avow that additional surprises are in the offing."

Moving a hand to her open mouth, Lady Simpson stifled a gasp.

Sir Henry grinned. "To settle your concern, I can also guarantee there will be no scandal. Quite the opposite, in fact."

From the small mezzanine balcony, a string quartet played a waltz. The floor cleared to make way for dancers. Gloved hands touching, couples swirled around the room. When the piece ended, conversation replaced the music until interrupted by Franz's strong voice.

Everyone turned, eyes upward, to see the Maestro and his lovely chanteuse standing at the mezzanine railing.

Franz took the lead. "Your Royal Highnesses, our gracious hosts, lords and ladies, honoured guests, there are several announcements to be made. The first is that the proceeds from this evening's concert will be matched by the benevolence of the Prince and Princess of Wales. This will provide the funds required settle all debts in regards to the reconstruction of the Theatre Royal, Covent Garden."

The crowd responded with strong applause mixed with whispers.

Marie-Fleuri scanned the attendees. Most eyes were fastened on her. Many didn't notice the swarm of servants carrying trays of champagne until the glasses were placed in their hands.

She kept her fingers clasped, her knees locked, willing them not to collapse.

When it appeared that everyone had been served, she nodded to Franz. He lifted his champagne. "A toast to Their Majesties, the Prince and Princess of Wales."

The guests echoed their response.

She filled her lungs, releasing the tension in her body with a controlled expulsion of breath. A demure smile in place, she made eye contact with individuals in locations around the ballroom. To some, she gave a slight nod.

When the voices stilled, she turned her focus to Franz. He returned her glance before addressing the reception. "I have asked a personal friend, His Grace, Bishop Blomfield, to come forth to make the next announcement."

Hand in hand, they stepped back.

The Bishop of London approached the railing. "Three weeks ago, I had the honour of performing a very special marriage. It was a small affair with only two witnesses in attendance. Allow me to introduce the newlyweds, Mr. and Mrs. Franz Stromeister."

A wind of whispers blew through the ballroom.

"I shall call upon Sir Henry Godfrey to offer a toast to the bride and groom."

Lady Simpson ran back to Sir Henry. "You knew! You were one of the witnesses, weren't you?"

He regarded the short, rotund hostess with utter dismay. "It would be proper protocol to complete the toast, would it not?" Glass raised, he bellowed. "A toast, then. To the happy couple."

The Bishop of London called for attention. "The bride and groom wish to address the assembly. It is my great pleasure to introduce Marie Stromeister."

She stepped forward. The room was so quiet she could hear laboured breaths coming from Lady Simpson, who now stood immediately below the mezzanine railing.

Marie curtseyed. "Your Royal Highnesses, Lord and Lady Simpson, lords, ladies and honoured guests. Thank you for your wonderful applause at the concert and for your gracious wishes for my husband and myself."

Franz resumed his place beside her and spoke. "Lord and Lady Simpson, thank you. I ask your forgiveness for not confiding in you. I wanted this evening's performance to be without expectation of my wife's vocal skills. I also did not want to take away from the most serious purpose of the concert, the new Theatre Royal, Covent Garden. For these reasons, Marie and I," —he cast a loving glance to his left— "needed to rehearse in isolation.

"If you will be so kind, please allow your guests to use this occasion to also celebrate our marriage. I know that each of you would like to offer your wishes individually, but..."

He nodded, and Marie addressed the audience.

"We request your understanding. Franz asked me where I would like to pass our first months as husband and wife. For personal reasons, I chose the Americas. We have passage booked on the steamship SS Great Britain. Our trunks are already at the wharf, and we must leave immediately if we are to join them."

They ducked through the miniature mezzanine door. The string quartet stuck up a waltz.

Sir Henry met them at the rear entrance, standing out of hearing range of the driver and footman. "Marie, you were sensational. Your performance was beyond reproach. I apologize for ever doubting that you and Franz were meant to be together."

She kissed his cheek. "Your concerns were justified. I still fear that upon our return, the charade will be discovered."

Sir Henry took her hands. "There is no need for concern. You were perfect at the concert hall and beyond perfection at the reception. You radiate grace and class. You spoke as one of aristocratic upbringing, and yet, did I detect a wee hint of colonial undercurrent? No, of course I do not expect an answer." He smiled. "On a lighter side, your presence has put Lady Simpson in an absolute dither."

He turned to Franz. "I shall write frequently, relating all rumours about your bride. Once the two of you have selected which details best fit your purpose, I shall propagate that version through gossips like Lady Simpson. When you return, Marie's background will be established and accepted. How will anyone doubt what they themselves created?"

Marie held out her hand to Franz. "Come, love, we have a ship to catch."

Sir Henry made a partial bow. "And I must return to the party. Lady Simpson already suspects me and my wife of being your witnesses. I do not wish Charlene left alone to be interrogated by her."

When Sir Henry reentered the ballroom, most of the guests were standing in small groups. Lady Simpson flitted from one circle to another like a voracious hummingbird in a tropical greenhouse, sampling whatever nectar she could before being drawn to the possibility of greater abundance at the next bouquet.

As she spun away from two couples, she bumped broadside into Sir Henry.

"How could they leave without giving me the opportunity to meet her personally?"

"It's rather plain to me," said Sir Henry. "They are living in a misty world of love and thinking only of their need to be together. Since the Prince and Princess do not appear to have any concern about their early departure, should we not show the same decorum?"

"But I don't even know her name or where she is from. Nor do I have any idea who her family is or what affairs they are party to."

"You most certainly do. Her name is Marie Stromeister. Her family is Franz, whom we know very well, and she comes to him from her heart. Regarding her affairs, given what I witnessed this evening, I believe she has established herself as the greatest performer in all of England."

"She did sing admirably," conceded Lady Simpson.

"Yes, that too," breathed Sir Henry, making his way back to his wife.

DADDY'S HOME

Her limbs shook like cold, wet leaves in a November wind.
She pulled her twisted sheet up over her clammy nightshirt
and hugged the stuffed bear she thought she'd outgrown.

Daddy's Home

Carly bolted upright.

The only light in the room was a thin white bar at the bottom of her bedroom door. Her limbs shook like cold, wet leaves in a November wind. She pulled her twisted sheet up over her clammy nightshirt and hugged the stuffed bear she thought she'd outgrown.

When will the nightmares stop?

She sank into the mattress. Her thoughts drifted uneasily. Neon flooded her mind's eye as shapes took substance.

An anxious voice called across the distance. "Get out of here. I said leave. Now! I'll call the police."

"You don't need to call anybody."

"Please...Steve. You'll wake the kids. Just go."

Carly jerked up onto her elbows. She strained to hear. Another nightmare? The voices always seemed so real, but....

"Steve, the judge said you couldn't come here."

"No judge can tell me to stay away from my family. This is where I belong."

Carly clasped a hand to her mouth. *My God, he's back.... He's in the house.*

The coldness left her. A fire of fear and anger took its place. Putting aside her bear, Carly lowered herself to the floor, crawled to the bedroom door and listened.

"Have you been drinking?"

"What if I have? A man's entitled to a drink now and then. Come 'ere. I wanna look at ya."

"Stay away from me." Her mother's voice stern but trembling.

Carly stood, back pressed against the door. *Doesn't he realize how hard this is on Wendy?* She whispered a prayer for her little sister. "Please sleep through this."

Wendy had been sent to the principal's office twice this month. When Carly got to the office the second time, Mrs. Smith explained that Wendy had hit another girl in her second-grade class. Once in the office, she hadn't stopped crying and begging for Carly.

Carly held her little sister and comforted her.

"I'm sorry," Wendy had sobbed. "Anna said my drawing was silly. She laughed at it. I hate her!"

"That's no reason to hit her. Just don't let her know it bothers you. If you don't get mad, you're the winner."

Hearing herself say that had almost made Carly laugh. She sounded just like Mommy. But, the laughter hadn't surfaced.

"I want Daddy to come home," Wendy had cried. "Why can't he do that, Carly? Why can't he come home?"

Carly had caught a tear of her own before it dropped on her sister's soft brown hair.

Her mother's voice jarred her back to the present. "Steve, I'm warning you. You have to leave."

"Now, come on. I just got here. How about we have a cup of coffee and talk a bit? The counsellor said we should talk things out."

"It's too late for talking. Get out."

Carly heard the slap and her mother's screech. She hid her face deep in her cupped hands.

"Get up and make my damn coffee."

Carly watched the scene unfold inside her mind, a video that wasn't supposed to play anymore, one she believed would never be seen again. The judge's words had locked it away.

Instead, the images slithered out from a corner of her brain.

She knew exactly what was happening in the front hall below her. Her mother would try to get up. Carly felt her mother's pain as he kicked her in the side. Now her mother would roll over and try to escape the next blow.

With blurred vision, Carly inched her bedroom door open. She had to get past the stairs without being seen.

It seemed to Carly that she was always hiding now. She would have walked smack into him one day last week if her best friend, Maria, hadn't warned her. Track and field practice had just ended. He'd probably been out there the whole time watching her. Just the thought gave her the creeps.

"Carly. He's outside," Maria had said, breathless from running to catch her.

"My dad? What am I going to do?"

"Go out the gym doors. My mom and I will pick you up in the parking lot."

That time, Carly had escaped. Still, every week, he was somewhere, although never at home. The judge had made it clear; he was never to go near the house.

Carly peeked downstairs. Her mother was curled up on the floor. Her father stood with his back to the staircase. She ran past the top of the stairs, fighting back more tears.

He snarled. "I'm going to see the kids. Move your lazy ass and get that coffee."

Carly ran into her mother's room, certain her pounding heart could be heard throughout the house.

"Hey, Carly, I'm home. Wake up, baby. Daddy's come to see you."

Down the hall, Carly's bedroom door creaked. She grabbed the phone off her mother's night table. It slipped through her trembling hands and hit the hardwood floor with a bang.

"Carly, where are you?"

Dropping to her knees, she grasped the phone and punched 9-1-1.

Her father filled the open doorway. "Why are you in our bedroom?"

She clutched the phone. Someone answered. Carly didn't wait for the woman to finish. "Three forty-one Oakwood Drive. It's an emergency."

Her father strode forward and grabbed the receiver. She fought for control, but her fingers burned as he tore the lifeline from her hands.

He covered the mouthpiece. Bringing his face close to hers, he rasped, "Now, why would you do that, Carly? I just came t' visit."

He slowly raised the receiver to his ear. "No, miss."

She saw his lips moving, but the voice flowed from another time. It was so gentle and confident. It was the voice that used to soothe her when she scraped a knee, the same voice that lulled her to sleep when she awoke from a nightmare. Now it *was* her nightmare as it erased her hope.

"No problem. Just a tween angry about being grounded, trying to cause a little mischief. Sorry for the trouble.... Yes, I'm certain.... Thank you. Goodbye."

Terrified, Carly watched him rip the phone line from the wall. She cowered below him, wishing for strength that didn't come.

He dragged the back of his hand across his mouth. "You're getting to be no better than your mother." As he turned to leave, he lobbed the phone over his shoulder. It hit the wall an inch from her left ear.

"Leave her alone." Her mother's scream came from just outside the room.

Carly grabbed the edge of the night table and pulled herself up. "It's okay, Mom. He didn't hurt me." She ran for the door as her father disappeared into the hall.

"Out of my way!" His loathing intonation stung her senses. A loud thud and a moan. Carly scrambled out of the bedroom.

Arms outstretched towards her, Carly's mother slid down the wall and collapsed on the floor.

Eyes foggy, stinging, Carly knelt and pulled her mother's head onto her lap.

Grunting, her father stomped away and opened the door to Wendy's room.

"Wendy, Daddy's home." He stepped inside and gave her a gentle shake. "Are you awake?" Her eyes opened." That's a good girl. Give daddy a hug."

Carly brushed back her mother's hair. "Mommy, are you okay? He hit you."

A swollen eye blinked open. "I'm fine, honey." The endearment wheezed through clenched teeth.

Carly helped her mother to her feet, and together they hobbled to her sister's room. Her father sat on the bed with Wendy snuggled in his arms. Carly hurt inside as she listened.

"Daddy, why don't you come home?"

"I am home."

Wendy touched his cheek. "You can't stay, can you?"

"No, I can't stay. Mommy won't let me."

"Daddy, I want to play in the park with you, like we used to."

"I'd like that too, sweetheart."

Sirens whined in the distance.

"Wendy, I have to go now." Her rocked her in his arms.

"Please don't go, Daddy."

"I have to."

"Why won't they let you stay?"

"Mommy doesn't like me seeing you. Tell her to let me come home. Will you do that, sweetheart?"

Carly watched him tuck Wendy back under the covers and give her a soft kiss. *How can he be so sweet and yet so terrible?*

He stopped at the bedroom door and stared at Carly and her mother. "I'll be back."

Carly fell to her knees and hugged her mother's shaking legs. She could hear him downstairs, running through the kitchen to the back door. Pulsing red and blue lights broke through the bedroom windows painting the wall above her. The doorbell rang.

"I called the police, Mommy. I got him to leave, didn't I?"

"Yes, darling, you did."

"But he said he'll be back. Mommy, when will the nightmares stop? I just want them to stop."

The Artist

...she pressed a thumb firmly on each drop, thus leaving the only signature she had.

The Artist

The dull ruby teardrop trickled down the surface of the painting. Its trail cut through the black, plumed fedora and across a dispassionate face illuminated by a fire's glow. Having lost too much of itself on its journey, it came to rest above a child's golden head. There it stayed, a worthless drop of life on a priceless piece of art, a natural blemish damaging a lifeless ornament.

She removed the crimson-soaked scarf from her slit wrist and sourced another flow of blood onto the most precious of her lord's secret treasures. As it settled near the fire's hearth, she pressed a thumb firmly on each drop, thus leaving the only signature she had.

With head tilted, she pensively stepped back from the easel to better assess her work. Then, careful not to damage her signature, her bloodied hands pressed back into the canvas. She smeared her pigment as deeply as possible into those of the original artist, trying to make the two inseparable.

Satisfied, she raised the silk of her full gown from the stone floor and walked across the hall to the massive oak doors. They yielded to her push, allowing her access to the dark and frigid winter's eve. After pausing to adjust, she strolled a short distance into the forest.

No longer part of his collection, she lay down and became one with the stillness of the night air. This time, her escape would be successful.

SWIMMING

Blueberry Island, our favourite picnic spot, got in the way.
It s become the backup destination on each attempt since.

Swimming

I'm swimming for my life, which is the story of my life. Just different strokes at different times.

I pull my right arm below the surface, the sidestroke, keeping my face above the water. How ridiculous is that?

Steve is the recipient of my most creative strokes. Straddling him. Plunging down. Slowly rising. Muscles quivering. Repeating until ready to explode. Holding off for the last tantric second when our bodies release in unison, in ecstasy.

But in love?

Or going non-stop, faster and faster, rolling over and under on his crusty living room carpet until our knees and elbows are chafed raw, burning with as much intensity as our hunger for each other.

How can I feel so sated and yet starved?

The snap of my legs propels me forward. I focus on the distant island that ended my first suicide—swimicide—attempt. The emptiness of the day after Grandpa Paul's funeral returns. It's a vacuum easily filled with images of the sorrowful, weepy drive ending at his vacant lakeside house. The idea had been to swim out until I was incapable of going further, to sink into oblivion. Blueberry Island, our favourite picnic spot, got in the way. It's become the backup destination on each attempt since.

His worn and kind face hangs inches ahead of me. When strength or spirit fails, when I can go no further, he'll be waiting for me. These silent words repeat with each kick of my feet and thrust of my arms.

The water is cold, even for September. My numb skin no longer registers the temperature, but the initial memory still shivers from the icy circles that crawled up my legs, meeting to form a figure eight, then morphing into a single loop over my hips as I inched away from shore, my toes instinctively extending my body upwards each time a wavelet crested. The porpoise-like plunge. The impact shocking my eyes and paralyzing my lungs until I broke the surface and stroked forward into the open water of Rice Lake.

A different cold. Home was where the heart wasn't. The only one not stoned or drunk by mid-afternoon, I left with bravado and hidden tears on the day after my seventeenth birthday. Different tears than the ones being washed away today.

As my right arm extends forward, I count the summers.

The first destination on my couch-surfing express was Steve's sofa. In some ways, it was too comfortable, at least for living with a first cousin. The next stopover was with his girlfriend, Sharon, followed by an eleven-month date with a hide-a-bed in a co-worker's trailer. Then back to Steve—his bed this time. All the while doing shift work at the Thickson Petro-Can, barely earning enough to keep the store-front loan sharks at bay.

Hard to believe it's been three years.

Dad hasn't called once. Mom remembers birthdays, not always sober and maybe not on the right day, but close enough.

Finally, a real job at the GM plant working the line. I allow myself a watery grin. Union qualification only six months away. And a small place of my own. Just a bachelor, but all mine, and walking distance to a pool.

But is it worth sticking around for?

I stop swimming before the lake deepens and the weed bed begins, crouching to keep my shoulders—and my questions—below the surface. Fingers roll into fists; elbows press against my bare sides, then relax. Eyes close. Aromas of pine, drying leaves and lake water linger—soothe. Arms and hands become weightless. Waves rock me like I'm still in Steve's solid arms, or like the endless swing of the pendulum hanging in Grandpa's ornate clock, only inverted, with fulcrum toes anchored into slightly shifting sand, while surface swells sway me to and fro, my head the bob, timeless.

Looking back over my shoulder, my shoes and clothes lie heaped and barely visible on the tiny beach where Grandpa and I built sand castles. Where he taught me to swim. Nothing left now but memories. The longing throbs inside my cold shell. I can't keep doing this. It *has* to be the last time.

The chill penetrates. My body shakes, but not only from the cold. Time to move. Knees bend and spring, another dolphin arc. The front crawl, my strongest, and good for a hundred metres. I ignore the pain and continue. My rules demand that each swimicide attempt be harder than the one before. I force my body to do an extra fifty.

Arms and shoulders ache. Legs are weak. Breathing is more like gasping. Time to switch strokes.

The breaststroke. My favourite.

Steve's fingers titillating my erect nipples. His palms warm, skimming just above the surface but close enough to brush the peaks of my arrhythmic breathing. The cupped hands, on their return, pressing and massaging.

My body shudders, moaning for more.

He'll be waiting, expecting me. Wanting part of me.

Three hundred rapid strenuous metres, my head lifting and mouth catching air with each synchronized pull of the arms. I stop, try to tread, my hands flailing against the surface. The burning and the weakness are telltale signs. Lactic acid is building in my limbs and shoulders. The familiar hint of nausea pokes around my belly. I swallow hard to keep it down. Cramps aren't far away. Maybe further than the island. Maybe not.

Doesn't matter. That sinking feeling moves in. My mind lapses into lethargic blackness. Why get out of bed to face another day? Why get out of the water? Who cares? Steve? Not likely. And one less present for mom to forget.

Staying afloat isn't what it's cracked up to be.

I float on my back, stomach rising and sinking—sinking—feet dragging it down. Almost vertical, I tread again.

No resting. That's the rule. Push to the island or surrender. One more hurdle to get under, then the final press.

Two surface strokes and a third down, bent at the waist, legs and feet swing upwards—a javelin pulled, rather than thrust, into the depths. Eight counted frog-kicks, arms and legs, drive me deeper into the peat-stained darkness. Forefinger and thumb pinch the nose. Ears adjust. Left hand stretches and sinks into the silty nadir of my upside-down hurdle.

Body pulls into a ball. Feet press into the muddy bottom. A comforting sensation oozes between my toes, tempting me to stay. Just take a breath, it coaxes.

I uncoil and thrust up. Arms extend overhead, clearing the way. Lungs ablaze cry to be replenished, but instead I continue to force out bubbles in measured amounts until the gauge hits empty. Lungs will the lips to part. Water seeps in, the taste fresh.

Consciousness wavers. A sense of calm.

Fingers break the surface, grasping air.

My chest heaves. Sweet oxygen rushes in.

Residual embers of anger ignite and burn deep inside. I had rolled away, twisted and spent in the sheets. Steve's grasp had engulfed me, had brought me back to him. His grip, like Grandpa's Conibear trap that hangs on the wall beside other forest souvenirs, able to stifle my life with a snap of my neck. I drifted into a nightmare, woke with a jolt and said, "I have to leave."

Steve kissed my forehead. She'll be back. It was in his eyes. It was in the shrug of his shoulders as he threw the covers aside and strode naked to the shower. It was because...*I always go back*.

The final press. An endorphin-laced fly, the most difficult, at a time when little is left. I count off fifty-four laboured strokes—the last two, open hands merely splashing, progress stalled, feet searching emptiness below.

Lips kiss water. Nose submerges.

Ahead, a water-blurred wall.

My nails reach and scratch, then dig into a crack in the granite oasis. I hang there for a minute, head tilted back, sucking air into my ravenous chest. Eyes squeeze shut. Hands feel their way along the shoreline, like fingers reading Precambrian braille, until they find a familiar handhold. They pull the rest of me onto the gradual slope of south-facing rock.

I roll over.

The fall sun wicks away the water and replaces it with warmth—like Mom did with my princess-pink bathrobe, before the booze took over.

Searching the seamless, azure sky, I absorb its radiant bliss. Every smouldering myofiber tells me the threat of drowning has ended—and—*I am not going back.*

THE DREAMER

For Emily, Whenever I May Find Her

*...we moved to the couch to watch Bogart and
Bergman in Casablanca....
For more than two and a half hours, I held her,
not wanting to break the spell.*

The Dreamer

For Emily, Whenever I May Find Her

I held her once. While I did, the lyrics to a Paul Simon song ran through my head in a continuous loop. The protagonist woke from a dream to find his lover beside him. He embraced her honey hair with thankful tears. Girl, I love you.

***

I told my buddy, Jim, I only wanted to get her into bed. If that had been true, I wouldn't have hurt so much.

To be honest, I was totally in love, incorrigibly in love, indisputably beyond hope.

Isn't that the bitch of it.

My car wouldn't start. I was bent over the engine like a dog burying its head in a food bowl. And there she stood, not ten feet away, grinning at the sound of my cursing. She saw me bang my head on the hood when I straightened up and heard me swear again. As soon as I refocussed, my heart stopped. My mind froze.

I ran a sleeve across my mouth, mopping away saliva leaking from the corner.

She smiled, held my eyes with hers, and then tossed mine away with a roll and a blink.

Ouch.

She headed up the street toward the Mady Centre. And what did I do? I stood motionless on the curb, like a statue waiting for pigeons. I watched her disappear from my sight.

I often thought about her, planning what I would say if I saw her again, thinking about how she would answer me, how I would take her in my arms and how she would finally kiss me. Three months of living contentedly in my imagination.

Daydreams are wonderful things until they end.

Living in the future of your own fiction is a drug. When reality crawls on top and inserts its life-sized stinger, you desperately try to dull the pain of what is with more images of what might be. You become addicted to your fantasy.

For three months, I was an addict.

Some might call it fate, others, the luck of the draw. Either way, it was an inconspicuous start. She was working at the same polling station as me in the basement of Grace United Church. Before the polls opened, those of us designated to work the tables convened to pick up our alphabetized electors lists. We introduced ourselves.

Emily. It was the only name I heard.

She and I headed to the table with a handwritten sign stating G to L. For a moment, I considered mentioning our close encounter. However, I gave it some thought before I spoke. Did I want her to remember that foul-mouthed fool who rammed his head into the car hood?

The long line of voters offered little chance for conversation. My contribution was seldom more than, "Here it is. This person is on the voters list." Ruler in place, I'd cross out the voter's name. Emily would then hand out the folded ballot and explain the voting procedure.

Each time I executed that ritual or said anything else to her, the subtle green of her hazelnut-flecked eyes would deepen to emerald. The corners of her ever-present smile crept a little higher.

Honey hair framed fine features, tumbled around her neck and ended in loose waves caressing her shoulders. Her cheekbones were slightly sculpted.

I tried not to stare. It was damn near impossible. She had an incredible figure—her v-neck top was conservative and revealing at the same time. My eyes tried to venture where they shouldn't go. Not cool, and at a minimum, I wanted to appear cool.

When the polls closed and the ballot boxes were dispensed with, several pollsters decided to go out for beer and wings. I waited for Emily's response and then agreed.

We grabbed a booth with two other workers. June was a large woman with bulbous eyes, a ready smile and a nose for sniffing out all the town's news. We'd gone to the same high school. From what I could tell, she hadn't changed much. George, I didn't know. He was at least six foot, had the handshake of a bear and a deep laugh you couldn't help joining. Emily was...well...she was beautiful.

"The first round is on me," George offered. No one protested. He signalled the waitress and ordered a jug.

June suggested a large plate of nachos.

Once the usual superficial information had been shared—Emily was a nurse at the Royal Vic—June jumped in on a fact-finding mission.

"Emily, you're the only one I don't know. Where are you from?"

"I moved here from Vancouver five years ago."

"Oh, I love Vancouver. I met David Suzuki in a restaurant there. Josh and I have lived here all our lives. We went to Barrie North Collegiate. He was quite the shy one back then." She laughed. "I had a tremendous crush on him, but he never responded to my advances."

Advances? I don't remembered saying more than hello to her back then. My surprise must have shown because June reached over and touched my hand. "Oh, come on Josh, remember the Spring Frolic dance in grade eleven? I asked you to waltz. It was a slow sexy one. I even pressed against you so you'd feel my breasts."

I did remember that. They were rather small.

"Instead of enticing you," June continued, "I think I scared you off. When the song ended, you headed straight back to the wall where your friend Jim was hiding in the shadows."

I was ready to crawl under the table by the time the nachos and beer arrived. George poured everyone a glass.

"Here's to you, Emily," said George. "I hope you're enjoying your time here."

We raised our glasses and drank. I started to ask Emily where she lived.

June cut me off before the second consonant hit the airwaves. "Emily, how long have you known Josh?"

"We've never met before today."

I drew a line through the condensation that had formed on my glass. As happy as I was that she didn't remember how I had embarrassed myself, I was devastated that she had no recollection of me at all. Our eye contact had been piercing; at least mine had been. Once again, I must have worn my reaction on my sleeve because June had no problem reading me.

"Josh, is she hiding something?...Josh?"

"No, she's right, we never really met,"

"Never *really* met? Hon, you either did or you didn't."

"We, ah, saw each other one day several months ago in passing." I turned to Emily. "We never talked. We kind of made eye contact."

Emily looked perplexed and then clasped her hand to her mouth. "You were arguing with your car. I think it was winning." She giggled. "That was you, wasn't it?"

I would've been happier if she had forgotten me.

She put down her glass. "I'm sorry I didn't remember you. I should have asked if you were all right. It was a little comical at the time, and you didn't seem to be hurt."

I didn't have to say anything. My burning face took care of that.

George cracked up.

June snorted in the midst of a mouthful of beer. After a gurgling gulp, she joined his laughter. Wiping a tear from her eye, she said, "It is a small world. Are you dating anyone, Josh?"

I shook my head.

June swung her gaze back and forth between me to Emily as if she was watching a tennis tournament. "Are you seeing anyone, Emily?"

"No, I..."

"Well, there you are, Josh. You're both available." June clasped her hands and sat back, obviously pleased with her matchmaking attempt.

Emily's cheeks flushed. She shifted a little in her chair. "Actually, June, I've come out of a bad relationship, and I'm not interested in dating."

"Nonsense. Fall off a horse and you have to get right back on." June volleyed her attention back to me. "It looks like she's as shy as you are, Josh."

"Or maybe she's not interested in a relationship at this time."

Emily looked at me, signalling her appreciation with a slight nod.

Within our mutual uneasiness, I saw both an escape and a possibility. I took a glimpse at my watch, and drained the remaining half of my glass. "It's later than I thought, and I still have to review some notes for a meeting tomorrow." I looked over to Emily.

She caught my glance. "I should be going too." She retrieved her purse from under the table.

I stood. "Can I walk you to your car?"

"Yes, thank you."

I put twenty dollars on the table. "This is for our share of the bill. Sorry we have to bail on you two. Nice meeting you, George. Good to see you again, June."

Outside, Emily paused. "Thanks for the rescue and for picking up the tab. I wasn't comfortable with the direction the conversation was heading."

I agreed.

Just before we got to her car, I built up enough courage to ask her out. After all, I had dreamed about this moment for three months. In spite of what she had said to June, I hoped that in private, a different answer was possible.

"I'm sorry, Josh. As I said, I've come out of a bad relationship. However, if you want to get together for coffee during one of my breaks and keep it light, that would be fine."

I tried not to show my disappointment. Still, you have to start somewhere, and although a crumb may not be as good as a banquet, it beats starving.

I shouted as she eased her Mini Cooper convertible away from the curb. "How will I find you?"

"Call the hospital. Ask for the maternity ward."

No hug, and certainly no kiss.

For the second time, I stood alone on the curb. At least drool wasn't dripping down my chin.

We met at The Java Haus.

Even in hospital garb, she was gorgeous.

I outdid myself in the conversation department. I was intelligent, witty, and surprisingly coherent.

Emily had the greatest laugh. Before leaving, she said she'd never laughed so much in her life. She gave me a light kiss on the cheek and another on my lips. Pure joy shone in her eyes. My heart was as vibrant as spring.

My confidence skyrocketing, I asked the question. She agreed to dinner on Friday.

That scenario played in my head a dozen times before we met for coffee.

Here's what actually happened.

I got to The Java Haus ten minutes early and was fidgeting—my nerves on edge. I watched several heads turn as she entered. She was even more beautiful than I remembered. However, it wasn't her appearance that grabbed me, or more precisely, knocked me back in my chair. It was her presence. She radiated warmth, caring, and sincerity.

I stood up to say hello, lost my balance, and tripped on the chair leg. It fell over.

I snagged the table with one hand, and managed to stay upright. We laughed, but it was forced. Two people trying to appear comfortable while at least one of them—me—was far from it.

I set the chair back up and turned it so she could sit.

"I'm buying. What would you like to drink?" I blurted out.

"Thank you. I'll have an espresso. I'm in the home stretch of a twelve-hour shift. I need some help to make it through the last four."

I ordered her espresso and a latte for myself while stealing glances at her from the counter.

Once seated, I asked, "So what do you do when you aren't nursing?" My right knee started to twitch violently. I slipped my left hand under the table and tried to hold it down.

"I like to golf and bike," she said, "although I don't have time to do either as much as I'd like. In the winter I downhill ski. What about you?"

I explained I didn't own a bike, but this spring I had bought a new set of titanium clubs that added at least twenty yards to my drive, and yes, I also liked to ski.

My knee stopped twitching.

We exchanged golf stories—worst chip, best drive, and most famous golfers we had met. We talked about where we had skied and where we wanted to ski next. Time flew by.

Emily stood up, flustered, "Oh my God! I'm late. Thanks so much for the espresso. Let's do this again."

And she was gone. No peck on the cheek. No kiss on the lips. Reality's stinger hit home. Still, she did say let's do it again.

I went golfing with Emily in beautiful Muskoka. After the eighteenth hole, we went to an elegant manor house for a drink and a romantic dinner. We retired upstairs, but instead of going into her room, she joined me in mine and never left. Again, this was what I dreamed would happen.

We did get together for golf, but not in Muskoka. We met at Landing's driving range in north Barrie, a few minutes from the hospital. Still, it was wonderful.

We laughed at each other's incompetence and congratulated each other on our occasional brilliant drives. Leaving the range, we walked hand in hand to the parking lot. Before getting into our respective cars, she leaned forward. Her lips brushed my cheek. Closing my eyes, I enjoyed the warmth of her touch.

She followed me to a roadhouse restaurant. Entering, I moved closer to her and touched her fingers with mine. Her hand drew away.

We took a booth by the window. I ordered the Burger and Brew special. She asked for a garden salad and Perrier.

The staccato sound of raindrops on glass drew her attention. "It looks like our timing was perfect."

Her index finger traced the path of a raindrop running down the outside of the pane. She turned back to me. "Thanks for coming up with the idea. Today was fun. You have a great sense of humour."

"I've never thought of myself as funny."

"You have a light side that's refreshing. And you have a great golf swing as well. I can't believe you had three drives top two hundred and fifty yards—straight down the middle. I'm lucky to get two hundred out of my swing."

"The guy next to us seemed to think your swing was better than mine. He studied every shot you took."

She smirked. "You mean Mr. Argyle Socks? You could tell he had a lofty impression of himself, but his performance didn't match his ego."

"Yeah, I thought it was somewhat droopy as well," I joked.

Her eyes widened. "You're bad. That's not what I was implying. I meant, his balls didn't get enough air."

I grinned and said nothing.

Emily blushed, laughed and covered her eyes. "That didn't come out right, either."

We both cracked up. Tears were flowing when the waiter arrived with our meal.

Over coffee, I asked if she'd be interested in going out again.

"I'd love to. But I still want to keep it light."

During the next month and a half, we became almost inseparable, enjoying each other's company more and more. True, we never held hands since that time at the driving range, and there were no more pecks on the cheek. Nevertheless, we were having the time of our lives. Long walks, trips to the beach, golfing, movies. We could discuss anything. We never judged each other. There was never a bad idea, just different ideas.

She emanated a sense of peace and playfulness that affected everyone around her. People's expressions changed from flat to high gloss as she spoke to them.

This was the person I fell in love with. Her physical beauty became the icing on the cake.

The more time we spent together, the more we laughed. The more we laughed, the deeper I fell in love. My feelings for her tunnelled deep within me.

Dreams four and up—I stopped counting—took us to a level of intimacy that she would not allow.

Give her time. Be patient. Those phrases became my mantra.

Then, there was a shift.

During dinner at my apartment, we killed a bottle of red. When the crème caramel was finished, we moved to the couch to watch Bogart and Bergman in *Casablanca*. For the first time, we snuggled. While Sam played 'As Time Goes By,' we slid down the couch, and I wrapped her in my arms. We lay together, my chest pressed to her back, our legs nestled together like two folds in a fan.

After the Lockheed Electra lifted off with Ilsa on board, and while Ricky and Renault evaporated into the mist, Emily's breathing became deep and smooth as she likely drifted into a dream of her own.

For more than two and a half hours, I held her, not wanting to break the spell, drifting in and out of my own slumber, never allowing myself enough time to dream. I felt every breath she took. Her body warmed my skin even through my shirt. Her hair smelled fresh. It shone as it blanketed the cushion. The full moon flooded the room.

Waking a little after three in the morning, she explained that she had to go. I walked her to the car. We held each other for what seemed like several minutes and then kissed. My heart opened wider than it had ever opened before. If ecstasy is a state of mind, my mind was well across the state border. It struck me at that moment that I had never known love before.

The next day, she dropped by to tell me she didn't have any romantic feelings for me, that the night before was fun, but not to read anything more than friendship into it.

We saw each other less and less.

Two months later, she called to say she was moving back west with her old boyfriend and she'd miss me.

Months later, I'm still alone.

And, I still dream.

Isn't that the bitch of it.

The Marksman

The bastard is somewhere in this alley. It's as if I can smell him above the rest of the garbage the summer heat is cooking in these huge rusted kettles.

CHAPTER 1

To move forward is to die. To stop is to die without meaning.

Chapter 2

"Sam, get your gorgeous butt over here."

"Is that any way to talk to your new fiancée?"

"It is when she's the most beautiful woman this side of the Atlantic."

Samantha walked over to Simon. She stretched up on her tiptoes, wrapped her arms around his neck, and drew his head down. Her lips brushed his, painting her words on his breath. "I love you. Simon Fielding."

She applied the final punctuation with her tongue.

Chapter 3

The pain and the damn blood won't stop. Everything's a sticky, greasy mess.

Chapter 4

Sam and Simon walked down Yonge Street, ignoring the people they passed on the crowded sidewalk. The heart of the city was where they most enjoyed their free time. Everything they relished was within easy reach. For them, the noise and energy of Dundas Square, its hawkers, buskers and vendors selling fatty street-meat, all melded into a perfect summer-in-the-city stew of smells, sights and sounds.

At the corner of Dundas Street, a sidewalk artist was putting the finishing touches on a full-sized drawing of Marilyn Monroe. She stood in her signature pose with her ivory cocktail dress puffed out above a real city grate. The grate let out a swoosh of air every time a subway train passed beneath it.

Sam circled the drawing. "Simon, come over here. From this angle, she looks 3D, like she's really standing over the grate."

She eyed the artist. "Can you take a picture of the two of us with Marilyn?" He accepted her smartphone. A mischievous smirk on her face, she stretched out on the dirty sidewalk beside the drawing.

Simon glanced around, his eyes wide. He touched his forehead. "What are you doing?"

"If we want to look like we're standing beside her, we have to get beside her. Come on. It'll be fun."

Simon scanned the people waiting at the corner for the light to change. Only a few were paying any attention to them. "Oh, what the hell." He laid down on the opposite side of Marilyn and blew her a kiss.

They changed their poses like fashion models while the artist snapped shots from different angles. More cameras and smartphones were raised as a crowd gathered for the impromptu show.

Getting back onto their feet, helpless from laughter, they dusted themselves off and staggered into the shade of the Eaton Centre to check out the photos.

"Nice legs," Simon said.

"Mine or Marilyn's?"

"Yours, of course." He pulled her close and placed his hands just below the cuffs of her very short shorts. He explored her eyes. To him, they were placid pools of speckled blue water, the calmest place on earth he could imagine.

Sam walked her fingers up his back, tracing each contour of muscle through his t-shirt, leaving a trailing wake of shivers.

"Thanks for not working today," she whispered. "I know the pressure you're under to get that proposal done over the weekend."

His lips brushed the top of her head. "I wasn't going to miss one of the few Saturdays you don't have to work."

She kissed his chest. "Since we have the whole day, let's go down to The Beach."

"As long as you're holding me, I don't care where we go."

They hopped on an ageing streetcar that lumbered past the eclectic shops on Queen Street East and continued over the Don Valley. Within twenty minutes, they were strolling along the boardwalk that bordered Lake Ontario. Stepping out of their running shoes and socks, they shuffled barefoot across acres of sand, passing a forest of volleyball nets and buff bodies. Veering down to the shoreline, they let the chilled lake water extinguish the fire that had built under the soles of their feet.

The day was theirs. The city was theirs. Love was theirs.

CHAPTER 5

The bastard is somewhere in this alley. It's as if I can smell him above the rest of the garbage the summer heat is cooking in these huge, rusted kettles. Somewhere, amongst the filth, he's licking his wounds and getting ready to move on. It's crazy, but I feel like I'm linked to him. It's how I know he's still here.

I can let him make the first move, or I can start down the alley and risk being seen.

As if the constant ringing in my ears isn't distracting enough, the growing sound of sirens is maddening. Where were they when we needed them? They can't do a damn thing now—which pretty much narrows down my options.

Chapter 6

The ice cream was cold and delicious. Lying on his back, Simon took a taste from his cone, a drop landing on his chin. Samantha licked it off.

"Do you want to try mine?" she asked.

He nodded.

She coated her lips with pink ice cream, leaned over Simon and kissed him squarely on the mouth, easing his head back into the grass.

"Mmmm. Now I know why it's called Strawberry Sensation," he mumbled. "What other flavours do you come in?"

She pressed her lips harder to his and stretched out on top of him. He wrapped her in his arms. Any residual tension Simon held inside melted away with the warmth of her body.

They lay motionless in the patchwork shade of a large maple, oblivious to couples walking hand in hand, cyclists and inline skaters streaking by, mothers who tugged toddlers and pushed carriages down the boardwalk, and soon oblivious to forgotten ice cream lost to the sun and the lawn.

CHAPTER 7

I can do this. *I-can-do-this.*

If I find him, I need the element of surprise. The bastard still has his gun.

The punk fired so many rounds on the street, it may be empty. I hope he has at least one bullet left. I want to kill the son of a bitch.

I keep pressing against the hole in my side, but it's like trying to fit an oversized cork into the neck of a shaken pop bottle. Instead of stemming the flow, the blood just oozes out around my hand.

A burning jolt sends my back into spasms.

"Shit! I can do this. Just please—God—stop the pain."

He doesn't.

Like it or not, it's time to move.

This side of the alley has a series of dumpsters between me and the next side street, a good two hundred metres away. I head into the alley and run along the rear wall of the cafe until I get to the closest dumpster.

I want to peek around the outside corner so I can look down the alley, but if he's watching for me or anyone else, that's exactly what he'll be doing. He'll see me first.

Instead, I wedge myself into the thirty centimetre gap between the dumpster and the cafe's brick wall, and edge deeper into the alley, into the abyss.

Chapter 8

Sam shivered. "I'm getting chilly."

"I'm not," whispered Simon.

Sam turned her head brushing her chin across his chest. "That's because you have this sexy, warm blanket on top of you."

He kissed and squeezed her. "I don't want to come out from under that blanket. Do you always look after your patients this well, Intern Samantha? I may have to break a leg and go to ER to find out."

"Don't waste your time. I save the best on my bedside manners for you, Mr. Fielding." She kissed his forehead and started to push herself up, but Simon drew her back to him.

"I think I fell asleep for a few minutes. I was having a wonderful dream," Simon yawned, "and I want to finish it. I was with the most stunning woman on the planet—that would be you—and do you have any idea what we were doing?"

"I know exactly what you were doing."

"And how would you know that?"

"Because not all your body parts were sleeping. If we weren't in public, I'd have taken advantage of you." She kissed him again. "But…you missed your chance. I need to get moving and warm up. The breeze is picking up and I'm cold."

Simon stretched his arms out across the lawn. "If we must."

Sam sat up, straddling him, her butt on his crotch, her legs folded on each side of his thighs.

Simon moaned. "If I were you, I wouldn't stay there too long. I may end up not caring where we are."

She leaned forward and gave him a quick peck. "I won't. I want to save it for when we have some real blankets."

"We won't need blankets tonight."

She smiled and stood. "You know what I mean. Let's go back downtown. I want to get that navy top we saw at the Eaton Centre. After that, a crisp Chardonnay at Rocky's Cafe patio would be nice…," she helped him up, pressing her chest into his as he rose, and kissed him, "…before heading home for dinner and…" she kissed him again, her tongue exploring his, "…dessert."

Simon gently withdrew. "I love you, Samantha. More than the world itself. I love you so much."

"I love you too."

CHAPTER 9

I make it through the space between the dumpster and the brick wall. The only additional damage is a scraped knuckle. The part of the lane I can see is empty, except for fast-food trash scattered around the stained asphalt.

The sirens have stopped. The paramedics are no doubt wheeling the useless stretcher out of the ambulance. I bite the inside of my cheek as hard as I can until it turns off the images.

I sop up my tears with my t-shirt, only to get a mixture of blood and sweat smeared into my left eye. A cleaner section of my shirt doesn't reduce the stinging. Worse, my right eye is watering so much, I can't see squat. I lose valuable time waiting for more tears to flush away some of the sting and the hurt.

The alley is deathly silent. I look out from the back corner of the dumpster. There isn't anyone else in sight. If he's still here, he isn't moving. So, I do.

I hobble ten metres to the back of the next dumpster, stop, and listen.

Like a giant rat looking for a rotten piece of human waste, I squeeze between the bin and the building.

A click.

Then a scraping sound like some little punk scuffing his shoe on the ground.

CHAPTER 10

Simon held Sam's hand as they threaded their way down Yonge Street. The sidewalks were busier than when they had left a few hours earlier. The afternoon shoppers and wanderers were making their way to parking lots, subway stops, and Union Station. Within a couple of hours, the flow of humanity would reverse, as replacements headed into the city's core for the restaurants and the Saturday night entertainment the suburbs didn't offer.

A cluster of people stood in a cloud of cigarette smoke outside Rocky's Cafe.

Five bandana-clad youths in baggy pants stood arguing at the corner of Dundas Square across the narrow side street from them. The youths made no effort to get out of the way when Simon and Sam approached.

Simon tightened his grip on Sam's hand.

The boys 'animated, profanity-laced debate, about whether to head through the square or go into the Eaton Centre, increased in volume.

Simon stepped onto the street and led Sam past them, keeping her to the outside. They crossed the sidestreet and stepped back onto the south curb, a few steps from the Rocky's main entrance. He turned towards the sound of screeching tires. A black Mercedes squealed to a stop. Its tinted side windows slid open. Two metal rods poked out from each of the dark cavities. Simon grabbed Sam and swung her towards the restaurant, placing himself between her and the car. Her face wore a twisted expression of confusion and shock. He pushed her backwards toward the doors.

Pistol shots cracked.

People screamed, scrambled.

Chips of cement flew through the air.

Bodies fell.

CHAPTER 11

The sounds from the other side of the dumpster have stopped, but their effect hasn't. My entire system has gone into overdrive. My heart is pounding, trying to break out of its cage. I lean against the bricks to let my energy build, realizing for the first time how tired I've become. There's increased dampness stretching down my leg as my racing heart accelerates the flow of blood from my side. I squeegee away as much as I can with the flat edge of my palm and shove some of my shirt into the hole with my baby finger. With the excess blood wiped on my shorts, I do what I can to take in a slow, deep, silent breath.

I inch my way between the wall and the dumpster until I reach the far corner and risk a glance.

He's about ten feet from me, sitting on the ground, peering around the front of the bin. He turns and leans against the metal side, stretching his legs in front of him. I pull back out of sight, breathe and steal another glimpse.

The gun is in his right hand. His head is tilted back against the dumpster. His eyes are closed.

He's crying.

His face twists. He bends his left knee, bringing his bloodstained pants toward his stomach. His right hand drops to the pavement. He puts down the gun, removes the bandana from his head, and wraps it around his thigh.

I take some change from my pocket, reach up and lob it over the dumpster, aiming for the middle of the alley.

I miss. A dull patter indicates that some coins land inside the dumpster, but at least a few make it over and clatter to the pavement. The bandana falls off his leg as he spins to the corner and stares back up the alley. I dive forward, crashing into him, blindly searching the pavement with my right hand, but the gun twirls out of reach. Instead of chasing it, I smash my fist into his head. I'm sprawled half on top of him before he starts fighting back. The little bastard's much stronger than I expected. We roll and squirm. He grabs my hair and yanks. My scalp ignites in searing pain. He bucks and twists. As I start to slide off, I hammer him again. My fist connects solidly with his temple.

I hold my breath. The gun is lying inches away, almost under his back. I grab it and press the barrel to the side of his head.

CHAPTER 12

"Move!"

Simon pushed Sam towards the cafe's door. He glanced back. "Christ!"

People were scattering. The Mercedes 'windows closed. Its engine raced. Smoking tires propelled the car up the street. Two of the bandana-clad youths lay on the pavement—one motionless in a pool of blood—one twitching and moaning beside him. Two others sprinted after the Mercedes, their drawn guns spitting bullets. A fifth kid ran in the opposite direction, straight toward Simon and Sam, his head turned up the street as he fired wildly at the receding car.

Simon yanked Sam away from the kid's path, but not fast enough. Still shooting, the youth slammed into them.

An explosion set off shrill ringing in Simon's ears. Samantha's body jerked…and went limp. Simon's biceps reacted, picking up the extra weight. A second explosion ripped a bloody hole in her neck. A fountain of blood squirted out, painting Simon's arm scarlet. Sam's head fell against his chest. His facial muscles turned to steel, his eyelids refusing to block out the horror.

The youth tumbled to the ground, releasing two more rounds and a shrill scream on the way down.

Simon cringed, a fire burning deep into his side. He slumped to the sidewalk. Samantha landed in a flaccid heap inches from him, inches from the youth.

The punk's expression was glazed. He got up, took a couple of unsteady steps, then limped away, gaining speed down the deserted side street.

Simon lifted his head from the pavement in time to see the gunman lope into the lane behind the restaurant, then turned his blurry gaze back to Sam. He sat up, pulled her to him, and rocked.

Her eyes stared past him.

He kept rocking, searching for a pulse.

There was none.

Twice, he forced his breath into her lungs. He checked for a response.

Saw none.

He laid her on the sidewalk, leaned over her, and pressed down thirty times in rapid succession. He felt for a heartbeat. Nothing. He repeated the procedure. Nothing.

Her halter top was torn and drenched with blood. He wiped away as much as he could from her neck. No new blood left the ragged, crimson hole.

He gave her more breaths. Pumped her sternum. He rested his forehead between her breasts and broke down.

He lifted his head.

Distorted faces stared through the cafe windows.

He cried out to them. "Help. Please. Someone help us."

No one moved.

Rage built like pressure inside a volcano. He stood and swung his head back, searching the clouds. A scream erupted from his core. He staggered along the side street to the back alley, ignoring the warmth flowing out from above his hip.

Chapter 13

Lying on our sides as if in a twisted lover's embrace, the punk and I stare into each other's eyes, our chests heaving with each breath we take. My arm is aching from its awkward reach. I carefully rotate my grip to reposition the gun backwards in my hand so my thumb rests on the trigger. I make certain the muzzle never loses contact with his head.

The kid, this killer, is probably no more than fifteen. The little bastard is shaking like a trapped rabbit. And so he should.

His teary eyes plead with me.

I picture Sam's beautiful face and eyes, and let myself drift into those calm pools of blue water.

Sliding the barrel of the pistol to the back of kid's skull, directly behind his forehead, I press my bloodied forehead into his.

I squeeze the trigger.

THE COLLECTOR

…she concentrated on the black handles protruding from the wooden block.… The counter edge dug into her belly. Reaching… stretching…one fingertip brushed a knife.

The Collector

"Girls, I'm home!"

Natalie closed her eyes and filled her lungs. The air was heavy with spices. Even the burgundy had released its subtle scent into the air. The slow cooker popped simmering suggestions of mixed flavours. The day's stress began to dissipate.

She entered the kitchen. The table had already been set. The four girls were at their places, ready for dinner.

"Sorry I'm late. You must be starving. I need a quick shower and then we can eat. It's been a rough day." Looking at the girls, she forced a smile and whispered, "But it's so worth it."

The shower was steaming. She stepped inside and slid the door shut. I can't believe Walter called a four o'clock meeting on a Friday. He knows I have to be home for the girls.

She scrubbed herself vigorously, trying to wash away the week's tension. The water burned a path down her spine. Shoulder muscles started to soften.

"Well, I'm not going to let Workaholic Wally ruin this weekend. I've been looking forward to it all year." She inhaled the moist air, counted to five and exhaled.

"If only Rick and I can work things out. Is that much to ask? He says he loves me."

She gave three rapid Lamaze-like puffs to release the stress, turned off the tap and pulled back the shower door. Cold air hit her. She shuddered, dried off with a bath sheet and wrapped it around herself.

Bound tightly, her eyes closed, the trapped radiant heat from her skin had a therapeutic effect. She stepped out of the shower stall and wedged her big toe under her underwear that had fallen onto the floor. With a quick flick of her foot, her panties flew through the ensuite door and flopped onto her bed.

"If it was only that easy to land a man."

She thought of her girls waiting for dinner and banished the frown. She towel-dried her hair in front of the mirror and tied it back in a ponytail. A rejuvenated face beamed back at her. Jeans and an oversized sweatshirt offered a welcome release from her restrictive business attire. The soft cotton touching her breasts was freeing and even a little sexy.

She went back downstairs to the kitchen. Barb and Millie returned her smile. Ronnie and Jess looked like they were sharing a secret. Natalie warmed some bread in the microwave, dished out some stew, and joined her girls at the table.

"Did you have a good day? Sorry I was short with you this morning. The four of you can play with Debbie and Sandy for an hour after dinner, but I don't want to hear any excuses when it's time for bed. Is that a deal?"

She took a spoonful of stew and let it hover under her nose for a moment before tilting it into her mouth. Her eyes closed. It tasted even better than it smelled. Her tongue sampled the flavours as if judging a fine wine. She swallowed. A satisfying warmth flowed down to her stomach.

By the time dinner was over, she was content, calm, and at peace with the world.

With cleanup completed and the last bowl loaded into the dishwasher, she poked her head into the family room and gave her daughters a half-hour warning for bed. With any luck, she'd have thirty uninterrupted minutes to read the newspaper—her evening ritual before tucking them in.

Being the eldest, Barb got to stay up an extra half hour to read or watch TV. The other girls didn't always like that, but tonight there were no arguments.

Once bedtime stories were read and the girls settled, she sank into the recliner in the den to call Fran. She smiled. There wasn't anyone in the world she'd rather spend this weekend with. How Fran managed to put up with her was a wonderful dilemma. Fran never seemed to tire of listening to her empty her heart, including the oft repeated vow to never forgive Tom for abandoning her and the girls. Not that he hadn't paid dearly for it. He had, inside the courtroom and out.

Subsequent attempts at a relationship all ended the same way. Once a man found out about her girls, he ran for cover. If there was a guy out there who wanted an instant family, she hadn't found him.

Through it all, Fran never complained. Okay, maybe she offered some unwanted advice now and then, but she never pushed the point.

Natalie pressed the video call icon on her phone. Fran picked up on the second ring, her fine freckled features and red hair filling the screen.

"Hi Fran. Are you set for the Brandie conference?"

Fran waved a mug with a picture of Brandie and Lenn on it. "Absolutely. Are you selling anything this year or just buying?"

"I'm going to see what I can get for my 1995 Happy New Year Brandie."

"You've got to be kidding. The one wearing the red, furisode kimono? I love her."

"I know, but she has black hair. You know me. Blonde hair and blue eyes, that's how she has to be. I heard there's a group of collectors flying in from Japan for the conference. I figured this is the perfect time to part with her." Natalie put on the widest, most devious smirk she could, then paused for effect. "Be prepared to eat your heart out. Whatever I get for her, I'm putting towards a 1998 Bill Massey Contessa Bride Brandie, but she has to be NRFB, never removed from the box."

"Oh my God. Really? She'll be a beautiful addition to your collection, sophisticated and elegant, but she's going to set you back a bundle."

"With the convention here in Seattle, what I normally spend on travel and accommodation I can use for the Contessa Bride. She's worth it. "

Fran pushed her lips out in a fake pout and pointed a finger at Natalie. "If you get her, I'll be jealous. I may never talk to you again."

Natalie laughed. "You'll get over it. I'll pick you up tomorrow morning on my way back from the gym. Is nine okay?"

"I'll be waiting, but don't expect me to be perky. I won't be through my first coffee by then."

***

The waitress stood beside the cluttered table, full plates in hand. "I hope you two ladies are hungry. We pride ourselves in the size of our portions."

Fran looked up. "You don't need to worry about that. We've worked up an appetite."

They gathered and bagged all the miniature outfits and brochures to make room for their pasta, which was placed steaming, in front of them.

Before taking her first bite, Natalie leaned forward in her chair and arched her back. "We must have walked five miles today."

Fran closed her eyes and sighed. "My feet will attest to that. We didn't miss a booth or a speaker. It feels so-o-o good to sit down." She raised her glass of wine. "Here's to the Contessa. She's beautiful. Where are you going to put her?"

Natalie glanced at the bag by her feet. "I think she'll look great in the family room's centre wall unit. She'll be able to see everything that goes on. Maybe it'll make her feel like she's holding court."

Fran tore off a piece of warm rosemary focaccia. "I had an amazing time today. I'm already looking forward to next year in Las Vegas, but it will be hard to beat this one."

"I agree. This was the best I've been to as well. The highlight had to be the Raphael Bellagamba's Brandie display. Can you imagine someone paying over two hundred thousand dollars for her?"

Fran shook her head, straight red bangs sliding back and forth across her forehead. "No doubt the rare Australian, purple diamond in her necklace had something to do with that. Where's the man who'll buy me one of those?"

Natalie frowned and stared into the distance.

After a few seconds, Fran waved a hand in front of Natalie's face. "Earth to Nat."

Natalie loaded her fork with spaghetti. "I can dream, can't I?"

"Sure, but getting back to reality, what did you think of the heritage display? I thought it was well done."

"I liked it, too. The old fashions were fascinating. It was like going back in time."

Fran ran a finger around the rim of her wine glass. "Can you imagine wearing some of those corsets? And what about having your husband picked out for you?"

Natalie's expression soured. "The results couldn't be any worse than they are today."

Fran looked up from her drink. "You've certainly had your challenges. Still, Tony might have been a schmuck, but he wasn't hard on the eyes. With his Grade A build and that amazing hair, he could easily have been a model for romance book covers." She broke off another piece of bread and soaked up some of the balsamic vinegar mixture sitting beside it. "C'mon, smile already. The Grade A comment was supposed to be a joke. Don't you miss him, even a little?"

"What I miss are the Angus steaks. Being married to a butcher had its perks." Natalie pushed spaghetti and red pasta sauce around her plate. "Let's talk about something else."

"All right. What about your renovations?"

"I'm only doing the kitchen. It will cost too much to take out the walk-in cooler that Tony built. Besides, it's great for storage."

"That makes sense. I know I could use more closet and storage space." Fran twirled some fettuccine around her fork, slowing as she spoke. "So-o-o...Nat, did you give Ricky the boot like you said you would? I don't mean to be harsh, but doesn't this make it three losers in three years since Tony?"

Natalie stared into her Chianti. "I seem to collect them, don't I? Maybe I should start hanging around more upscale places." She looked back at Fran. "I haven't given up on Rick, though."

"Are you crazy? You said he hit you."

Natalie looked away. "Well, he tried to, but he was hammered. He gets a little obnoxious when he's drunk."

"Sounds to me like he's always drunk."

Natalie's tone hardened. "We all have our problems. He's an only child. His parents are gone. He just needs someone who cares for him." She looked directly at Fran. "He told me he's going to quit drinking."

"Right, and I'm the Virgin Mary."

"He says he likes kids. I'm..." Natalie's voice tensed. She stared back into her wine glass. *How can I expect Fran to understand?* She cleared her throat. "I've decided to give him one more chance. I'm meeting him Thursday night at Taps in Boiseyville."

"In a country bar? You said he's going to quit drinking."

"He's proving it, by meeting me there and only having coke."

Fran sneered. "Probably the kind you snort. Ah, Nat... be careful will ya? Just promise me, if he screws up on Thursday, you drop him like a rock."

Natalie closed her eyes, raised and then lowered her shoulders. "Okay. I promise."

***

Natalie wedged her subcompact car between an extended-cab Ram and a jacked-up Ford 350. She opened the door and slid out. The air was thick and damp. Distorted neon rainbows, spelling Cold Beer, Hot Women, Music, and Pool, shimmered off the hoods and curved fenders of the parked cars and pickups. The lot was full, which was good. The more people, the less chance of being noticed if things didn't work out between them.

With optimistic and pessimistic thoughts battling for dominance, she took a deep breath. A shiver ran across her back. Tonight was the night. He was either a keeper, or he wasn't. It was that simple. She hobbled across the gravel lot, her stiletto heels challenged by the potholed, gravel surface. At the door, she smoothed her low-cut linen top, and gave a slight tug on the hem of her short red skirt.

She entered, squeezing between mostly male bodies. A Toby Keith lookalike touched her shoulder with a cold bottle of Bud. "Let me cool ya'll down a bit. You're so hot you're gonna set the place on fire."

She brushed the bottle off her shoulder and pushed on through the crowd.

It took a minute of searching. Rick was leaning over the bar, laughing at something the bartender was saying. She came up behind him, put her hands over his eyes and nibbled on his ear.

He turned. "That tickles."

She kissed him, then recoiled.

Rick tugged her towards him. "Don't stop. That was real nice." His eyes scanned her—head to toe and back up again. "You look amazing."

Natalie pulled back. "You taste like booze. You said you weren't going to drink tonight."

"I'm not. I had one last Jack before leaving home, a toast to sobriety. I'm on cola now." He held his glass up to her lips.

She sniffed it and took a sip. A second sample resulted in a smile. "Okay. Just remember. No more booze for the rest of the evening."

"Scout's honour." He put on a goofy grin and made a mock salute. "Now, my gorgeous lady in red, how about some VIP time on the dance floor?"

Natalie grabbed his hand.

He slipped from her grip and shouted over the band's opening chord. "Let me pay for my drink. I'll catch up to you."

She wormed her way through the crowd.

The bartender slid three vodka shooters across the mahogany surface. Rick glanced over his shoulder before downing them in rapid succession. He made a display of finishing the rest of his cola, swishing each sip around his mouth. He followed that with a mint breath strip.

The band's female lead singer encouraged everyone to dance or sing along.

Natalie turned at the sound of Rick's voice behind her. She eased up to his chest, and they drifted into the rhythm of Black Velvet. Her hands dropped from his shoulders to his lower back. She snuggled up to him.

They alternated between the dance floor and the back wall furthest from the band, with a few breaks outside so they could talk without shouting. Around eleven, the band took a break. She pressed her lips to his ear. "I know it's early, but I have to head home. I promised Barb I wouldn't be any later than eleven thirty. You can come over for a coffee if you want."

Rick ran his fingers through her hair. "Sounds good, but I haven't got my license back. You'll have to drive. I can take a taxi home from there."

She gave him a long kiss and traced his lips with her tongue. "Only if you decide to go home."

"What about your girls? Will they be in bed?"

"Barb will be up. She's babysitting tonight, but if we're quiet, she'll be asleep in a few minutes. Besides, I want you to meet her, and see the others. They're part of the package. You can't have me without them."

"I'm sure I'll like them. They sound like great kids."

A warm, buoyant sensation rose within her.

When they reached the exit, he kissed her. "I need a piss. All this pop is going right through me. You get the car. I'll meet you outside in a minute."

He worked his way along the bar towards the back hall. A wink to the bartender brought three more vodka shooters to the counter.

***

The dashboard clock read eleven twenty-nine when Natalie pressed the remote for the garage door. "That's cutting it close. I can't expect the girls to come home on time if I don't set a good example."

They went into the house. He steadied himself at the kitchen entrance.

She touched his shoulder. "Are you all right?"

"Ya. Caught the heal of my boot on the step. Lost my balance for a moment. I'm fine." He looked around. "Nice place."

"I'll give you a tour later."

Rick took her in his arms.

She nudged him away with a whisper. "Not yet."

Natalie opened a cupboard and leaned forward over the counter to grab a bag of dark roast. A hand massaged her butt. She gave him a punishing glance. "Hands off the merchandise."

The coffee maker filled, she placed two large cups on the counter. "Come on. I want you to meet Barb. We can tuck her in and read her a story. You can see the rest of my sweethearts, and then…." She winked. "The coffee will be ready, and we can get comfortable."

Rick followed close behind.

Fingers slid down her hip. She brushed them away. "Not until the girls are asleep."

She rounded the corner into the family room. "Barb, I want you to meet someone special."

Rick glanced at the TV—which was on—scanned the leather armchair, the sofa, and the fireplace. His eyes returned to Natalie. "Where is she?"

"Right here." Natalie ran to the couch and picked her up.

A puzzled look crossed Rick's face. "That's a doll. Where's your daughter?"

"This is my daughter, and she isn't a doll, she's a Brandie." Her smile broadened. Her voice became playful. "I got her when I was seven. She was my first girl, and she's still my favourite, although I don't let the others know that." Natalie cocked her head. "Is something wrong?"

"Ahh—no."

"Come on, we'll look in on the other girls."

She left the room and stopped in the hall. She turned. Rick was staring at the Contessa, who was beautifully displayed in the wall unit. His head was nodding.

He may be Mr. Right after all. She bounded up the stairs.

He followed.

An index finger to her lips, she eased a bedroom door open and signalled Rick to come forward. "Aren't they beautiful? They look so innocent when they're sleeping."

He leaned against the door frame beside her. "How many do you have?"

"Twenty-two. I adopt a new one every year." She looked down at Barb nestled in her arms. "Barb has been a wonderful big sister. She's a terrific help."

"Do they all have their own beds?"

"Yes."

"And different names?"

"Of course."

He took a step back into the hall. "Of course, they do."

Natalie tucked Barb into her tiny bed, lifted a Roald Dahl novel from the bookshelf, and sat cross-legged on the floor.

She held up the book. "We're almost through Matilda. Barb loves it." She adjusted the small comforter covering the doll. "Don't you, darling?" And started to read.

Rick remained in the hall. She motioned for him to come in. He hesitated and grumbled.

She paused at the end of the paragraph. "What did you say?"

"Um. Ya sure. If this is the drill, I'm good."

He tried to sit, lost his balance, and almost landed in her lap. His arm around her, she snuggled into him and continued reading. His hand slid over her top and groped her breast.

Natalie lowered the book and pushed him away. "Stop it. Not in front of Barb. What will she think?"

Rick rolled his eyes. "She's a damned doll. She can't think."

Misery cut through Natalie's heart. *He doesn't understand. I was sure he was different from the others.*

He leaned in, his other hand reaching up under her skirt.

"Rick. Stop."

"What's the matter? You were hot and horny back at the bar. Let's get to it." He twisted, placed a hand on each of her shoulders and forced her to the floor.

She squirmed. Before his lips found hers, she pushed at his chest. A twinge of pain spread out from her shoulder blade. His weight pressed down. "Rick. Stop. You're crushing me. Please, not like this. Not in front of the girls."

The pressure on her chest eased.

He sneered. "Loosen up. We both want this. What's the doll going to do? Get ideas and fuck Lenn?"

He laughed and dropped back down, his hardness evident. Her arms strained. His weight bore down on her chest. His left forearm pinned her to the floor. His free hand flew down her thighs, fingers grabbing the hem of her skirt. His mouth sucked the air from hers.

Her lungs convulsed. A laboured breath drew in some relief. She clenched her fists and pummelled the sides of his head.

He shifted slightly.

Air flowed. She hit him again and bit his bottom lip. He screamed.

A drop of his blood hit her cheek. "Get off of me."

He sneered and tugged harder at her skirt. "Not a chance. I'm gonna get what I came for."

She threw an awkward punch into his chin and drove a thumb into his eye. He howled, clasped his face and rolled. She shoved him aside, got to her feet and ran. One foot through the door, her upper body stopped with a lurch, his fingers digging into her right shoulder. She dipped and reeled. Drove an elbow into his side. Teetering, one hand pressed over his eye, he grabbed her arm. She broke free, sprinted away from the bedroom, and raced down the flight of stairs. His footsteps and cursing followed.

She glanced over her shoulder.

He launched himself forward.

She grabbed the bottom stair post and swung around it like a door on hinges.

Rick snagged her top. He crashed to the floor.

She spun, tripped over his body, managed to stay upright and sped into the kitchen. A howl followed her. She lunged at the sink. Grabbed the tap for support. Before she could breathe, he was there. Fingers grasped her bicep and yanked. Like stretching and releasing an elastic, she held tight, resisting his pull, then let go of the tap, spinning around, using the resulting momentum to drive a foot into his knee. Her elbow smashed his cheek. He buckled, fell and latched onto her ankle.

Her right foot immobilized, she leaned over the counter and focused on the knife block in the corner.

Nails clawed up her bare leg.

Ignoring the horrible sensation, she concentrated on the black handles protruding from the wooden block. The counter edge dug into her belly. Reaching… stretching…one fingertip brushed a knife.

An arm wrapped around her waist and wrenched her back.

Her fingertips closed on air.

Rick's right hand slid up the outside of her thigh. A finger hooked the waistband of her panties and yanked down, stretching the fabric at an angle across her rear.

Twisting, she saw he was on one knee, his legs splayed. Raising her left knee between her body and the counter, Natalie delivered an awkward backward kick to his groin. It lacked power, but his hold loosened.

Pushing up on her toes, pressing her left hand down onto the counter, she lifted and propelled herself across the it's surface, her right arm fully extended. Her palm felt a knife's handle. Fingers closed.

She felt herself being dragged her back. She went willingly.

The knife slid from the holder, the handle firmly in her grip.

Feet back on the floor, Natalie swivelled and leered down at him, each audible puff of her erratic breathing slower than the one before, like a locomotive pulling up to a platform.

"I thought…," a puff, "you were…," another puff, "different…You said you liked kids." The words were exhaled more than spoken. "I thought we had a chance to be a family. But you're just like all the others."

Rick released her leg and staggered to his feet, his bloodshot eye swollen, his face ruddy, fists tight, nostrils flared. A bull ready to gore. "You're fucking crazy. You don't have daughters…just chunks of stinkin 'plastic."

She watched his gaze follow the steel blade wavering in her hand.

He wiped saliva and blood from his chin. "I'm out'a here. I don't want nothin 'to do with you. You're…"

"You're not leaving me." Her hand steadied. Breathing slowed. She fed on the fear in his eyes. Her voice dropped to a low growl. "No one walks out on me and my girls. No one."

The butcher knife swung over her head and sliced downward. The blade dug into his shoulder, jarring in her hand as it deflected off bone. He stood frozen, disbelief written across his face. His hand went for the knife.

Natalie ripped the blade out. A line of blood followed its path across his palm. He stared at it and staggered. She drew the knife back, turned the blade horizontally, and plunged it into his chest. He sank to his knees, one eye wide open. Falling sideways, his head slammed against the ceramic tiles. The veins in his neck bulged. He coughed. Blood and pink foam pooled around his mouth. A puddle spread onto the floor from his chest. He flinched. His lips moved.

Leaning against the counter, her lungs heaving, Natalie waited until his body was still.

Grabbing the dishcloth from the sink, she wiped up as much blood as she could, then pulled one towel after another from a drawer until each turned crimson. When the drawer was empty and most of the blood sopped up, she removed his blood-streaked shoes. She went to the linen closet and returned with a sheet, which she rolled him onto. Wrapping the top two corners of the sheet around her, she dragged his lifeless body to the basement stairs. Struggling with the weight, she elevated his torso and descended backwards, one step at a time, his heels thudding against each tread. She lugged him across the rec room and into the walk-in cooler. After arranging his corpse in a sitting position on the floor, she rested his head on the shoulder of another, whose hollow-cheeked face was grey and gaunt with death. She nodded at a third cadaver, wearing a sports coat, sitting with its back rigid against the opposite wall, its mouth open in a grotesque grin.

Natalie relaxed, her breath visible, suspended in the frigid air.

She picked up a brush from a shelf and stepped forward to comb what was left of Tony's long black hair. The pressure caused the dried and shrivelled carcass to sway gently on the meat hook suspended from the ceiling.

She spoke in a sing-song voice. "No story tonight, boys. Ricky was bad. You need to learn how to be nice to girls."

On the way out, she lowered the temperature setting for the cooler. She returned to the kitchen, scrubbed and bleached the floor, the basement steps and the path to the cooler. With the knife washed, bleached, and resting safely in its varnished holder, she trotted upstairs to check on the girls, wiping down the walls and railings on her way. Stepping into the bedroom, she placed her right palm over her heart. Fortunately, the commotion hadn't woken them.

After showering, she sat down at the kitchen table, a cup of coffee by her side, and scrolled through the entertainment section of the local paper. She stopped at an ad for Josey's Red, White and Blues. The best Blues north of New Orleans. Dress to impress.

"This looks interesting. I really do need to start looking for my Lenns in more upscale places."

BODY ART

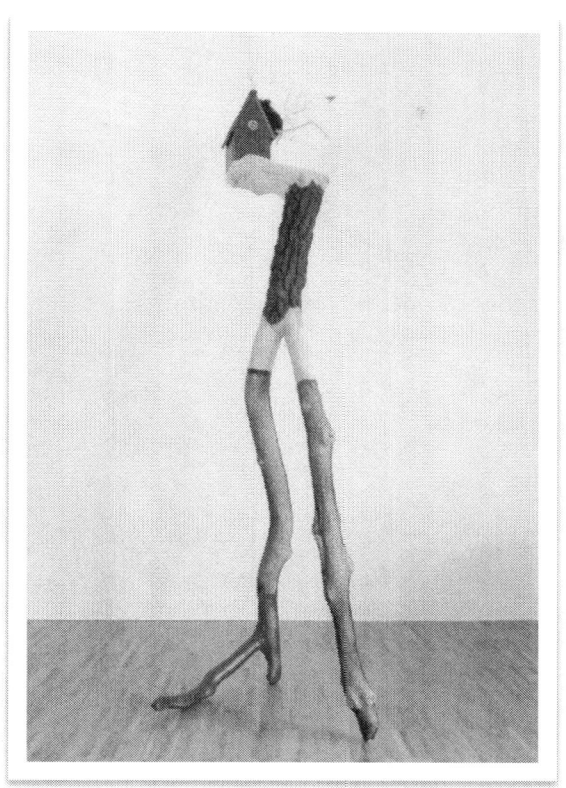

*Inspired by The Fascinator,
2015, sculpture by Toronto artist Sally Thurlow
Photograph by Ian Mackay*

Body Art

Few of the original strain remain. Fewer every year.

Genetically modified, our resistance to disease is now inbred.

Prenatal options are extensive. Post-birth alterations unlimited, and for the most part, unrestricted. Regulations, however, do not allow the removal of the individualistic nature of our brains, so creativity, innovation and subjectivity flourish.

While plastic and ink enabled our ancestors to sculpt and paint their exterior, gene manipulation addresses the complete being.

Self-expression has become rampant. Some view us as freaks, others as living, evolving works of art.

The vanguard has always felt scrutiny.

IN CONCLUSION

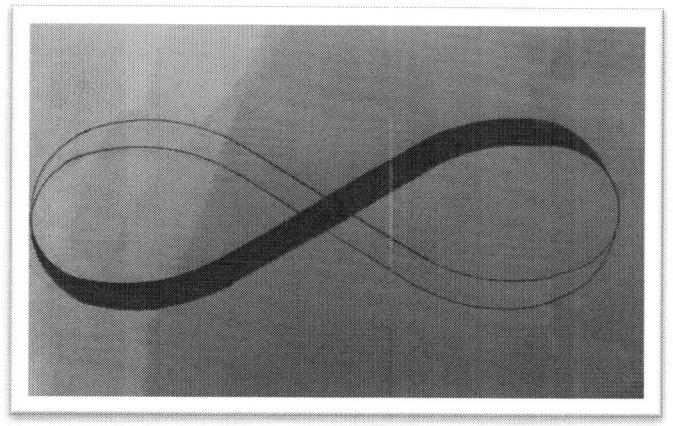

entwined in a journey, we'll all meet one day.

In Conclusion

Twilight is melting, chastising the day
Darkness is rising, repenting our stay
Night time crying
pleading
sighing
driving our dreams away.

A lover is dying to get on her way
Another is trying to lengthen her stay
All the time crawling
falling
calling
stepping on glass all the way.

By the tree was a soul who longed for a saviour
In the house was a child who yearned for a favour.
The saviour came and lifted that soul
A mother held the child from the cold
Lovers loving
leaving
dying
entwined in a journey, we'll all meet one day.

Author's Notes

—Inside A Twisted Mind—

The intent of this section is to give interested readers some behind-the-scene views. I ll begin with a short description of my writing process, followed by the inspiration for each story and any second-level message, should there be one.

If my explanations match your interpretations, that s great. If you took away different meanings or had different thoughts than what I offer below, that s fine as well.

My Writing Process

Originally, I believed the process had to begin with an idea. I always thought an author had to have the plot figured out before he or she put pen to paper or fingers to keyboard. An outline had to be created; the main characters had to be identified; the character s traits had to be documented, and other steps had to be completed. Once that was all done, the writing could begin. Many authors use variations of this process very successfully.

However, for me, no matter how hard I thought about it, my mind remained void of good ideas, my feet remained planted in the starting blocks, and my hands remained firmly buried in my pockets.

How did I finally start writing my first piece of fiction? I did it by following a suggestion from an acquaintance. I believe this process also kept me on track while avoiding the hurdle called writer s block.

I want to caution new and would-be writers that getting a story down and completed, although a huge accomplishment to be celebrated, should not be confused with the craft of writing—the quality of what s been written.

Here is my writing process. I take a few full breaths to relax. A short meditation clears my mind and moves me into a deeper state of relaxation to allow me to become one with what I call my inner, unlimited creative ability. After three or four minutes, I count myself back up to full consciousness, repeating in my mind that I will still be one with my creative ability. Upon reaching ten , I take a good stretch, place my fingers on the keyboard and write without thinking about what I am writing. If I am continuing an in-progress story, I will usually read the last two or three paragraphs before I start writing.

Writers like me, who write without a plan, are called pantsers", meaning they write by the seat of their pants." I prefer the term improvisational writers or improv writers.

When I first started using this process, I had no idea what I was going to write about before I started to type. Now, I often have a specific topic, idea, or like Stephen King states in his book On Writing, a question in mind. I never concern myself about plot or character development in the first draft. I let the characters tell their own story. Research also waits until after the first or second draft, by which time I know what I need to research.

With this understanding in place, I will take you through each of the tales in this collection and point out the inspiration, if any, that got me going. Before doing that, however, I will discuss a second point related to my writing process: the existence of a second level of interest in some stories.

In grade school, I always got annoyed when my English teachers asked the class what an author meant or what the author was trying to tell us. I wondered what the point of writing a book, a scene, a poem or a short story was if a reader needed to take a course to get the answer to that question. I didn t have much patience or vision when it came to reading.

Now, I sometimes find myself guilty" of stuffing extra meat between the layers of noodles, although not always intentionally. I guess it goes with the territory.

Here are a couple of examples from the world of music to help explain what I mean.

I was listening to an interview with singer songwriter Bruce Cockburn. He explained the origin of his song Wondering Where the Lions Are. It turns out he had a recurring dream about lions. Then the dreams stopped, never to return. Thir disappearance was the inspiration for the song. Not exactly life-altering, but who would have thought?

Another example is Paul McCartney s Blackbird. I listened to that song hundreds of times, not knowing its meaning, until I heard Paul explain in an interview that it was about the civil rights movement in the 1960s. When I hear either of these songs today, I listen with a different perspective. For me, that makes the experience more complete.

For those of you who want to know if there is anything extra in a story other than what first meets the eye, read on. If, at this point, you do choose to keep reading and discover that you received different interpretations than I describe, that is fine. In fact, it s great. It means the story got you thinking. Also, I don t claim to have all the answers. Remember, these stories wrote themselves. I just supplied the keyboard and display.

If you don t wish to read further, that is also fine. I believe these stories stand tall without trying to read between the lines. I sincerely hope you enjoyed this book and the characters you ve met.

I have received mixed responses from Beta readers on whether I should include the following section or not. Some view it as insulting". They don t want anyone telling them what their interpretation should be or what they should think. I fully respect their view. In fact, I agree with it completely.

Others, like me, as described in the previous discussion, want to know what the author s inspiration was and if the author has additional thoughts that may not always be obvious.

If you fall into the first group, please stop reading here. It is not my intention to force anyone to change or modify their interpretation. Above all, I do not want to tell people what think to or to annoy anyone.

If you fall into this second group, read on.

SPOILER ALERT:

Do not read further before finishing the book. This section discusses things that will ruin some aspects of some stories if read first.

If you do read what follows and if anything is left unanswered, contact me and let's have a positive, non-combative discussion. I may or may not have the answers.

THE INSPIRATION AND STORIES BEHIND SOME OF THE STORIES

Twins

I wanted to write about a set of twins, one evil, one good (nothing too original). Other than that, I had no idea where to start or what would happen. As you now know, their relationship was…well…different. Jeannie carries a burden of guilt for things that were not of her making.

There are hints to this in the story. If you wish, take another spin through it. Let me know what you find.

I didn't see any of them myself until I read Twins in its entirety after completing the first draft. Even I was surprised by their special connection when it flowed onto the screen at the end of the first draft.

This adventure of discovery is one of the many things that makes writing exciting for me

The Salesman

I admit to borrowing the concept of a body being kept in a bathtub filled with ice. It came from a novel. Which one, I can't remember. If I knew who the author was, I would give him/her full credit for the inspiration. All that remains in my conscious mind is that scene. I loved the visual, together with the nagging residual question of what would make someone want to do that.

Years later, when I sat down to write about a corpse in a tub of ice, Hank the salesman introduced himself. I didn't know anything about Hank at the time. How was I to know that he would fall in love with her? In fact, I didn't realize it was love until one of my early readers told me. I decided she was right.

Your interpretation is also correct, if you disagree with me.

It's pretty disgusting if you ask me. Who comes up with this stuff?

The Salesman tends to be one of those tales that people either love or love to hate .

The Order

I wrote this for a flash fiction contest, 500 words or less. "Secrecy" was the theme. I later expanded it for another contest, 1,000 words or less. (I didn't win either.) The story, which could take place in the present, the past or the future, is about one person's successful attempt to escape life in a cult

The story, which could take place in the present, the past or the future, is about one person's successful attempt to escape life in a cult.

On a deeper level, it is a discussion about trading off values, and in particular, ethical values. The story asks the reader which value, loyalty or secrecy, is more important, and should either trump honesty or freedom?

The unasked question for the reader is: "How do you resolve a dilemma created by having to choose between conflicting values, and in particular when one or more of those conflicting values are ethical values?"

This is the dilemma that Salacia presents to Jonas, forcing him to make his decision. Do you think he made the correct ethical decision?

Regarding the writing process, I have committed a near-mortal sin for writing short stories. For those of you who write, you will likely be familiar with the concept of Point of View or POV. Some purists say that a short story needs to be written from a single person's point of view, or at least each chapter should maintain a single point of view. Nothing can be shown, discussed or presented that the protagonist does not personally see, hear, feel, taste, or think.

This story is told from Jonas 'POV—who speaks on behalf of The Order—until the second-last paragraph, that is. It then switches to Salacia's POV. Interestingly, I did not so this intentionally.

I think it is only fitting that we should begin to see the world from her point of view at that moment in time.

(I have broken the single POV guideline in other stories as well. I'm such a rebel.)

Some readers, upon finishing the story, have asked me if Jonas lives or if he dies. Although readers are entitled to walk away with their own interpretations, the following excerpts may help explain my understanding.

Salacia tells Jonas that she returned to save his life.

Jonas submits himself to the Ritual of Cleansing (painful punishment), but not the Force of Loyalty (the furnace). The last sentence reads: "Today's secrets would be theirs alone."

I had an interesting experience after someone read the first draft of this story. She congratulated me on my choice for the female protagonist's name. This comment caught me completely off guard. I'd made the name up—or thought I had. Instead of admitting that I had no idea what this reader was talking about, I succumbed to pride and vanity and said nothing other than, "Thank you." As soon as I got home, I Googled "Salacia". In Roman mythology, Salacia was a female divinity of the sea. King Neptune wanted to marry her. To keep her virginity, she hid from him in the Atlantic Ocean. In the end, Salacia did agree to marry Neptune and share his throne.

Somewhere in the recesses of my subconscious, I must have stored away that name.

Does this link to Roman mythology suggest a future sequel in which Salacia and Jonas reunite as Salacia and Neptune did?

Hold on, wasn't Jonas also the name of a guy who had a whale of a time in the ocean?

Another coincidence?

Unrelated to this story, Salacia is also the name of something else. Any guesses?

The Saviours

As my early readers did not understand the deeper message in this story, I changed the title from The Saviour to The Saviours. By making the title plural, I hoped some readers would question who the "saviours" were and possibly see some of the following parallels.

The surface story is that of Clay and Georgina, their lives, their chance encounter and the outcome of that encounter. The words tell that story. The second level portrays the hypocrisy that builds over time within organized religions. This is what I set out to write about. I chose Christianity only because that is how I was raised.

It is not religions or their founders I critique here. It is the followers, who years or centuries later, do evil things. I know that in every religion there is a very positive caring, loving, spiritual and heroic side, one that is exhibited time and time again by many, many followers. But that's not the side of religious practices that this story is about. This story is about what happens when people create or fall into the dark side of religion.

Despite the strong positive values of Christianity's founder(s), what followed, in part, was power, perversion, greed and hypocrisy: the Spanish Inquisition, the burning of supposed witches, excommunication for believing the world was round, the Crusades, Protestants killing Catholics, Catholics killing Protestants, the unreported deaths of aboriginal children in residential schools, and on and on it goes. Summing it up: abuse, bullying, mutilation, killing, killing and more killing, all in the name of a god. Yes, this is the cynical view. However, the story's ending may convey a message of hope for humanity.

Who are the Saviours? There are three of them: Jesus Christ, Georgina's grandfather and Clay the slave. The parallels are as follows.

The first Saviour is Jesus Christ ,who created, or at least his followers created, Christianity—the Church. The foundation of the Church was built on very important, positive values. Christianity was established after Christ gave up his life to save the souls of God's "children".

The second saviour in the story is Georgina's grandfather. He built the new church in their new settlement and later risked his life to save it and the villagers—including his family—from a devastating flood. "He told the congregation that God spared their church because of the community's love for its fellow man." Despite the strong values that this little "church" was built upon, the enslavement of other people and the killing of an innocent man who saves a member of that church is accepted without question by some of its parishioners.

Clay is the third and most obvious saviour of this story. Just as Jesus died to "save" God's children, Clay puts his life at risk to save the grandchild of the founder of this community's church. Like Jesus, he is murdered in spite of, and partly because of, the good he has done.

At the end of the story, there is hope on two levels. By sounding his whistle, we know that in his heart, Clay has escaped slavery and obtained true freedom through death. Referring to the beginning of the story, we were told: "One day, when he was truly free, he would blow the whistle loudly and clearly."

Depending on your beliefs, you can interpret this as Clay entering eternal life with God, his soul being freed from this earthly plane, or his attainment of freedom from oppression—or however else you please.

Georgina also gives us hope. Despite her upbringing that taught her slavery is acceptable and that murdering an innocent person of a different race is justified, deep inside she knows it is wrong. She hasn't fully recognized it yet, but the knowledge is there. As stated, "Somewhere deep inside, she felt a pang of guilt but couldn't grasp the reason. She hadn't done anything wrong."

If you didn't get any of that from the story, you are in good company. Few do. In fact, one of the judges who awarded this story an Honourable Mention suggested that the title be changed to The Runaways, as the story had two runaways: Clay and…the horse.

Regarding the writing process, I set out to write a story about hypocrisy within religion. That was it. No outline, no characters, just that idea. Clay introduced himself in the first sentence.

It wasn't until after the story was completed, the singular version of the title assigned, and I had read it a few times, that the parallels became apparent to me.

I felt the surface story about Clay and Georgina stood well enough on its own, so rather than spell out the deeper meaning, I decided (like Garth Brooks 'song) to bury the axe but leave the handle sticking out—in case someone might want to grab hold, give a good yank and discover what existed below the surface.

The Unknown Civilian

The title is inspired by The Unknown Soldier. This story is not meant to take away from the sacrifice made by those who died at war defending our freedom. The intent is to add to that memory by recognizing the many civilians who fought and continue to fight tyranny; civilians who paid the ultimate price as a result.

This story of genocide could take place in any war-torn country, and therefore, the location is not given. On one level it is about a teenage boy who has watched the destruction of his town and the killing of his family by the army. In the end, he does what he can to fight back.

There is another layer in this work, told by the symbolism contained in his daydreams.

The daydreams speak to the irony that surrounds the perversion of political and military power within society. The boy symbolizes society. Society produces many good peaceful players as depicted by the small, harmless cloud animals which the boy—society—creates.

Every society also produces a head of state and some form of military to protect its citizens. In too many instances, one of these entities, as symbolized by the eagle, goes rogue and turns on all, or portions of, the very society that sourced it. The justification for the ensuing slaughter may be for any number of reasons such as honour, security, religious beliefs, cultural purity, etc.. It really doesn't matter because none of those are the real reasons for the butchery, nor would they justify war and killing even if they were. The real reason boils down to personal power, wealth or both.

Some individuals will always stand up against tyranny and fight back, but all too often, they die in their efforts. In many cases, the only witness to their stand against these madmen is the sun, moon or stars that watched over them. Their stories are seldom known, let alone told. This story is in memory of them.

The Performer

I started writing this story during one of my youngest daughter's violin concerts while waiting for her to come on stage. I did not set out to write about a violinist, but the connection to the concert is not surprising. When my young performer took her place in the spotlight, I closed my computer, somewhat relieved, as the story wasn't flowing well, or so it seemed to me. More precisely, it was out of character with my previous writing. I almost trashed it. I'm glad I didn't.

The only social statement in this story is the ridiculous notion of self-importance and superiority that people develop within a class-structured society — effectively, all societies.

The story ends with Sir Henry's double entendre.

Daddy's Home

This story was inspired, for lack of a better word, after hearing an acquaintance relate her personal nightmare. Her ex-husband was stalking her and her daughters,

Years later, I sat down at the keyboard, and Carly, Wendy and her mother told me their story.

Although Daddy's Home is a totally fictional account, I believe the story represents the abuse too many women, children, and sometimes men, suffer at the hands of those they rely on, those who claim to love them. It also highlights the uselessness of our legal and justice systems when it comes to protecting those most at risk. As some frustrated readers have pointed out, it doesn't end with a solid resolution. Those readers said they would have preferred to have had closure.

Wouldn't we all — but too often, that's not reality.

The Artist

There is nothing hidden here. Idiscovered several people took away a completely different meaning than what I thought was conveyed in an earlier version. As a result, I modified one word to help clarify that the protagonist was flesh and blood and not a ghostly spirit as some thought.

Regarding the writing process, I wrote this story as the opening to what was going to be a novel involving reincarnation—which this story ended up NOT being about.

I modified the first page of the first chapter to stand on its own in order to submit it to a "postcard" short story contest (500 words or less). I ended up liking it so much, I threw the rest away. I think the meaning of the story is self-explanatory. There is nothing hidden, at least not that I have discovered so far. If you see more to this story, I would love to hear your thoughts.

The Dreamer —*For Emily, Whenever I May Find Her*

Josh's unrequited love for Emily.

The story references two songs written by Paul Simon.

The Dreamer's subtitle is the song title, "For Emily, Whenever I May Find Her", a love song beautifully sung by Art Garfunkel.

The opening paragraph references the ending lyrics

of that song.

There are also references to the Simon and Garfunkel song, Wednesday Morning, 3 A.M. The song's protagonist is lying in bed awake. Having committed a crime, he must leave his love and flee. Her hair, lit by the moonlight, covers the pillow like a mist. Josh leaves Emily at roughly 3 a.m..

Unable to hold the woman he truly loves, the subtitle, For Emily, Whenever I May Find Her, implies to me that Josh may spend the rest of his life looking for his "Emily". What does it mean to you? Let me know.

The Marksman

I wanted to experiment with a story's timeline. I also wanted to write about the violent tragedies caused by gangs on city streets.

When I opened my eyes and started to type, Samantha and Simon walked off Yonge Street and onto my laptop screen.

In Toronto, where I used to live and still love to visit, innocent people have been in killed in drive-by shootings or by being caught in the crossfire of gang shootings. One such tragedy happened at a desert restaurant, another on Yonge Street and another in a large shopping centre. Unfortunately, this is not the end of the list.

On a different topic—and for the record—I wrote the

last scene of this tale long before the James Bond movie "Skyfall" came to the silver screen. I didn't use the movie as a prompt. However, since a draft of my story was floating around the USA, maybe my story inspired Bond's writers. I can only dream of being that influential and of one day having my name in the credits of some movie.

The Collector

A woman I once knew collected a certain brand of dolls and referred to them as "her girls". That caught my attention. From there, my imagination took over. No, she did not have a walk-in cooler. Every aspect of the story is fictional .

Upon reading the story however, she asked that I change the name of the protagonist, so I did.

Body Art

Why have people throughout existence painted their skin and pierced body parts for decoration and expression?

Why do some take it to the extreme?

How will these tendencies reveal themselves if or when genetic modification and gene splicing become available to the general public?

This piece of "nano fiction" was inspired by a sculpture by Toronto artist Sally Thurlow .

In Conclusion

This poem is intended to be a summary of these tales with a sense of resolution.

I expect that we have all experienced the pain of lost or misplaced love. We have all suffered at the hands of others, be it a sibling, a relative, a bully, a racist, criminals or war. I believe we have also all experienced the joy of love and the sacrifice others have made in order to help make our lives, or the lives of others, better. This poem reflects on human relationships by referring to characters in this collection. It is also about each of us.

The first stanza is about dreaming which is a common thread throughout this anthology. All the key characters have wishes and dreams, some achieve their dreams, some don't.

—We all have dreams.

The two lovers in the second stanza are The Artist and Marie-Fleuri, respectively.

—We are also lovers.

In the final stanza, the soul by the tree is Clay hoping for a saviour to arrive.

—That soul and wish is inside each of us.

The child in the house is Wendy, asking for what can't be, but finding warmth in the arms of her mother.

—Inside each of us, a child calls out.

Ultimately there is hope, hope that we will find our

lover, our saviour, our protector, and most importantly ourselves, and that we will find the first three in the form of someone with whom we will share mutual respect and love throughout the remainder of our lives, and possibly beyond.

Finally, the pain we inflicted upon ourselves and upon others, and the pain which others may have inflicted upon us, will constitute lessons learned. We will realize that when we hurt others, we harm ourselves. In the end, we are not separate. We are all connected. We are one.

***

Thank you for coming along for the ride. If you like what you read, or if you didn't, please leave a rating and/or a review on Goodreads.com, your countries Amazon site, Barnes and Noble, Indigo, or wherever you source your books.

If you are a teacher or in a book club, would individually publishing some of the stories with teaching notes be of value.

Bruce A Hanson

Instagram: @author.bruce.a.hanson
Goodreads.com
Web Site: bruceahanson.com
Email: bruceahanson.author@gmail.com

ACKNOWLEDGMENTS

The transition from dream to reality for this anthology has been a long journey with many changes, revisions and help from many people. To my "beginning of the journey" editor, Cathy Witlox, a big thank you for helping to add a touch of continuity and finesse to the earliest stories in this collection. Thank you to Cori Hanson for typing up an early draft of the manuscript from a printed copy after my computer went missing. To Bob Orth, a huge thank you for cleaning up the grammatical side of the collection—after which my many revisions introduced more clinical that would send shivers up his spine. Thank you to fellow members of the Barrie Writer's Club for their ideas, fine tuning, and significant reframing suggestions on all stories. A special thank you to author Susan Swan for her valuable suggestions and encouragement on The Dreamer. Thank you to Marylin Lamb for her "middle of the journey" line edit. Thanks to additional editors Rachel Churcher and Tracey-anne Platter. (If there are any errors in the book at this point, they were introduced by more changes I made, post edit or by those nasty typo-goblins that sneak into books in the middle of the night and wreak havoc.)

Thank you to Sally Thurlow for the inspiration for *Body Art*, and to both her and Ian Mackay for allowing me to include his photo of Sally's sculpture. Thank you Karrie Barnum for your artwork in Twins. Thank you, thank you, thank you to all my Beta and ARC readers: Julia Blake, Nannette Kreisman, Raymond Holmes, Karrie Barnum, Steve Ryan, Bruce Meyer and Tristan Ryan.

ABOUT THE AUTHOR

Bruce Hanson resides in Ontario, Canada balancing his time between Muskoka and Barrie, his family and writing.

His writing credits include:

1st Place (2021) - The Muskoka Author's Association

1st Place (2021) - The Royal Canadian Legion Branch 270 Senior Literary Contest

2nd Place (1998) - The Brendon Donnelly Award For Children's Literature

2nd Place Tie (1996) - The Mississauga Library Writing Contest

Honourable Mention (1998) - Canadian Author's Association CanWrite Short Story Competition

Honourable Mention (2002) - CAA Winner Circle 10 Inter'l Short Story Comp.

Long-listed (2015) - Ontario Writers Conference Story Starters Contest

Bruce has travelled quite a distance from his analytic Engineering roots. An introvert by nature, he stepped way out of his comfort zone taking improv acting from Second City, Toronto. He has appeared on the Cottage Life television show *Cottage Cheese*, and has worked as a Background Actor for TV and film including *Flashpoint* and *Warehouse 13*.

OTHER BOOKS BY BRUCE A HANSON

Glistening, snow-covered forest trails may look like a winter wonderland, but a forest can also hide secrets from the past.

Matt, a fun loving high school student, joins his twin sister, Ashley, and their best friend, Saadia, for a weekend of snowmobiling and cross-country skiing. Their first outing takes them to the site of a recent explosion where Matt stumbles upon a small gold cross emblazoned with a fleur-de-lis.

A retired curator identifies the origin and true value of the cross. That night, the cross is stolen. The three teens have their suspicions about who the culprits are, but when they go back to the explosion site to look for clues, they set off a chain of events that puts all their lives in danger.

For Ages 9 - 90

It's an animal invasion!
What's a boy to do?
He can always run to Grandma's house for shelter...or can he?

Under the pen name Robert Rime
For Ages 3-7

Manufactured by Amazon.ca
Bolton, ON

36139229R00150